THE LONG ROAD TO LOVING MITCHELL

ALICIA HOPE

Sometimes what a girl needs can be right in front of her....

Fires, violent storms, vandalism, and governmental whims are just a few of the issues Libby Barnes has to contend with after taking over the family farm in the picturesque lower south of Western Australia.

Loneliness is another.

Being young and unattached, she's also the subject of ongoing critical scrutiny by the ranks of doubters in the small farming community. Then a handsome stranger arrives on the scene, and Libby is no longer alone.

But will this new man in her life prove to be an asset, a hindrance, or merely a distraction?

And will he be there for her when disasters strike?

DEDICATION

*For readers of romantic rural stories.
And with heartfelt thanks to my wonderful, eagle-eyed beta
readers Jill and Heather. x*

ABOUT THE AUTHOR

Once you choose HOPE anything is possible....

Despite living within cooee of the Great Barrier Reef, idyllic tropical islands, and a well-stocked ocean pantry, author Alicia Hope is a self-confessed landlubber and disliker of seafood (I know - what the heck, right?!). She's also a keen horse rider, bass player, and bird watcher, and shares her gumtree-dotted acreage home with an author husband, Frank H Jordan, a feathered larrikin, cockatiel Kewbie Kewberton, and a whole bunch of wild birds, roos, goannas, and pretty-face wallabies.

Her feel-good stories showcase Alicia's love of the land and the natural world, and this is especially true of her LONG ROAD series.

For the latest on her books and writing life, visit Alicia online at aliciahopeauthor.blogspot.com.au, and collect an exclusive gift when you sign up for her oh-so newsy newsletter. :-)

1

'Oh hell.' The silhouetted figure backed away, arm raised to shield his face as bright, newborn flames streaked through the dry leaf litter, licking at the trunks of karris in the dense eucalypt forest. 'The gate valve ... you forgot to open it and the pressure's blown out!'

A cacophony of flappings and flutterings, alarmed bird calls, and undergrowth rustlings joined the crackle and hiss of the blossoming fire.

A second figure leapt back from the blaze as his shocked brain registered a strange, chill dampness at his feet. After an urgent scan of the pocket of recently cleared ground, he rasped, 'Ethanol. It's ... it's ... *everywhere*,' and dropped his panicked gaze to his feet. 'My joggers are soaked in the stuff!' Jerking up his head he yelled, 'We gotta get outta here!'

'So much for your design "improvements" to the still,' the first man snarled at a third, motionless figure. 'Now you've started a bushfire, you *idiot!*' He swept an arm to indicate their leaf-littered surroundings. 'And with all this fuel load, there's no way we'll stop the fire spreading.' Spinning on his heels and yelling over a shoulder, 'We've gotta go!' he scarpered for the safety of the forest and its deepening late afternoon dimness.

A safety that wouldn't last long, and a dimness already pierced by the glow of encroaching flames.

Darting across to clutch at the arm of his motionless friend, the second man yelled, 'We have to get out of here, mate. NOW, before we go up too.' When his friend remained rooted to the spot, staring horrified at the spiralling flames, the man shook his arm and shouted in his face, 'Come *ON*. Leave the still, we can't save it. We need to go. Now, now, NOW!'

At more loud popping and a burst of sparks from the intensifying blaze, the man finally moved, wincing as the rising heat radiated against his already flushed face. Still staring wide-eyed at the fire, he took a stumbling step backward before turning and dashing after his fleeing buddies.

Was that smoke rising in the distance?

No one would be stupid enough to burn off in this weather, surely.

Libby Barnes pursed her lips.

It was probably just Wal, getting rid of some more dock from his front paddock. Although, according to Dave Barnes, burning only goes so far because, '... dock must be pulled out by hand if you want to be truly rid of the damn stuff.'

The invasive weed was a headache for every farmer working land in the lower south of Western Australia, and elsewhere too no doubt. Libby couldn't even guess at the amount of time she and her parents had spent ripping out every patch they could find on the farm.

Totally worth it, though. We got rid of the 'damn stuff', saving ourselves thousands in lost grazing ground. And it hasn't come back, so I guess Dad was right about the best eradication method.

Right about that, and lots of other things.

She let the book she'd been reading—trying to read—drop to her lap. After allowing a precious hour in a busy day to lose herself in a story, she'd struggled to become engrossed. This was no reflection of the author's skill, the fault lay in the grasshopper antics of her own mind. There's always so much to consider, account for, plan, and worry over when managing a farm.

Especially when going it alone.

Heaving a sigh, she scanned the late afternoon sky.

Apart from the column of smoke, the only break in the cloudless blue expanse was the dark body of an eagle coasting lazily on air currents.

A decent fall of rain would relieve the summer stress on the land.

She closed her eyes to picture the paddocks the way she loved them best—green and awash with water during the winter rains.

An out-of-season downpour isn't too much to ask, is it?

Waving away moisture-seeking black flies, she squinted at the surrounding landscape. Brown grass swayed in the warm breeze, the clumps thin in places and dotted with patches of bare, sandy soil like old scars on the skin of the earth.

Her brow puckered.

The hot, dry Western Australian summers are simply part of nature's rhythms, was what her father had drilled into her. 'Land needs a dry season in order to sweeten and prosper,' was his standard response whenever she complained. 'Too much rain can have a souring effect.'

Like too much time alone can sour a heart.

Hit by the now familiar sense of isolation, of a piece missing from her life, she was glad when a muffled thumping from the round yard broke her train of thought. The sound also disturbed the snoozing cat, who raised his tabby head from off the veranda pavers, ears alert to this interruption in the hush of warm afternoon.

Sitting straighter in the sun lounge, Libby reached down to scratch the soft greyness between the cat's ears. 'What d'you reckon is making that noise, Sam?'

His throat rumbled into a pleased purr amid more thumping.

Libby slid her dog-eared bookmark into place. 'Guess I'd better go find out.' After wriggling her socked feet into a pair of well-worn riding boots she rose, gazing thoughtfully across at the cattle yard. 'I think it's coming from the trough.'

Sam too was on his feet, luxuriating in a full body stretch of his furry greyness. He sauntered after her, following as far as the post-and-rail fence, one of his many scratching posts around the farm.

After a quick manicure, made all the more satisfying by the stripping of some loose bark from off the post, he climbed up to stretch his lean tabby body along the top rail, a favourite vantage point. From there he could watch the grass below for movement worthy of a predatory pounce, or give an inquisitive horse's nose a playful, claw-free swat.

Leaving him watching her through half-closed yellow-green eyes, Libby made her way to the old bathtub that served as a water trough, one hand raised against the glare and her steps crunching on the dry grass.

As she drew near, her head shot up at the sound of splashing from inside the trough.

Something in there? A bird? A black cockie maybe?

A flock of cockatoos had arrived earlier in the day to slake their thirst at the trough. Screeching lustily, they'd congregated in a long line on the fence, preening their glossy black feathers and the flashes of white or red plumage under their tails.

Drawing closer, she gauged the water level in the tub.

Not deep enough to trap an adult cockatoo, unless it were injured of course.

She craned forward, and a glimpse of black and white greeted her before disappearing again below the rim.

Not a cockie. A magpie?

Edging nearer, she peered into the trough. Sure enough, a partially submerged young magpie gazed dolefully back at her.

Spurred to action by her arrival, the bird scrambled and flapped against the steep sides of the watery prison, clawing with strong feet, grappling for a foothold on the smooth enamel surface. Discouraged, it slipped into the water again. Panting and beating its soaked wings in frustration, it eyed her suspiciously while struggling to stay in the tub's shallow end.

With a soothing, 'Shhh ... you're okay, maggie. I won't hurt you,' she gazed down at the prisoner. 'You've got yourself into a pickle, my little black-'n-white friend, taking a drink from the slippery edge of a deep container like this. Then again, I guess your other water sources are all drying up.'

The poor thing's exhausted. He'll eventually drown if I don't help him out.

She squatted on her haunches, running over rescue options in her mind. It wouldn't work to simply grab the stressed bird. Not realising she was trying to help, the magpie would fight her with all the strength of its powerful beak and claws.

She raised a hand and waggled her fingers.

And I am kind of fond of these.

Dropping her hand to her side, she rose to circle the yard, searching as she went.

There's gotta be something I can use as a birdie life raft.

Only cleared ground greeted her, making her wish she'd left the usual assortment of farm paraphernalia lying around.

Was I a bit hasty, clearing the place so thoroughly when I took over the farm?

Hang on....

Did I just step over something for the second time?

Glancing back, she saw the long, heavy wooden pole used for closing off the fenced yard.

Sometimes what we need is right under our noses....

Indifferent to the splinters hiding in its rough strips of bark, she grasped it and, balancing its weight in her arms like a pole-vaulter, slowly approached the trough.

The magpie watched her with wary eyes but didn't stir.

Pleased the bird wasn't growing more agitated, she rested the heavy length of timber on the tub's edge.

Once I position the end of the pole in the water, the maggie can use it to climb to safety.

She began manoeuvring the end of the pole into the furthest corner, only to halt with the tip barely breaking the surface when the magpie, as if understanding the stranger's intention, calmly clawed its way on board. With most of its body now free of the water, the bird firmed its grip and settled itself on the pole, like a gymnast on a balancing beam.

For a long moment they stared intently at each other, black eyes locked with hazel. Libby knew that to the magpie she represented danger, so having the bird place its trust in her at a vulnerable time brought a deep swell of emotion and a connectedness she had rarely felt before.

With a glad smile and only a few wobbles along the way, she carefully raised the pole and its passenger. The bird appeared content to keep to its perch as it was borne upward, away from the water's deadly embrace. Once the pole's full length was resting securely on the edge of the trough, Libby let it go and straightened, beaming.

My good deed for the day.

Appearing otherwise unharmed, the magpie remained where it was, busily preening and drying its feathers.

He's not worried about me being so close. It's as if we've formed a bond of trust.

With a quick check to make sure Sam kept his distance from the soaked and still vulnerable bird, and finding the cat engrossed in something moving in the grass below, she squatted on her haunches to smile with simple joy at her new feathered friend.

She would have made the moment last longer if not for the jangling of the landline from inside the house. Rising slowly she backed away, took one last look at the contentedly preening bird, and then turned and jogged to the house.

'Hello, Boronia Station?'

'That you, Libby?'

'Yeah. Who's this?'

'It's Mac.'

Warren MacIntosh, the local fire chief.

Her thoughts flashed to the smoke she'd seen earlier, and her stomach lurched. 'What's up, Mac?'

'Bushfire,' he said urgently. 'We've got a crew on site fighting it, but with the wind blowing that way, it could come close to your place. You might want to consider evacuating.'

'*Evacuating?* Is it really that bad?'

'Has already consumed old Reg's shed and outbuildings. Right now we're working to save his house.'

'Oh no.' Libby's anxious frown deepened as she pictured the elderly Reg Edwards. His house was a shambles, probably the least valuable asset on the extensive grazing property, but it was the frail old man's treasured home. And while the farm was untidy, overgrown, its broken-down yards strewn with farming equipment, it was nonetheless worth many hundreds of thousands of dollars. And hadn't Reg grumbled to her recently about the insurance company's refusal to renew his policy?

Her stomach fell further as other thoughts raced through her mind, tumbling over themselves. One of them stuck its head above the others.

A fire's threatening and here I am, alone, with SO much to do before I can even THINK about evacuating....

'Oh, I nearly forgot to tell you,' Mac barked. 'MJ reckons he'll be over shortly, to help you get the stock and other things sorted in readiness.'

As Mac hung up, Libby blew a breath through pursed lips.

I'm not entirely alone.

She dropped the receiver back in its cradle.

I have MJ.

He rolled up a short time later, dressed in overalls and work boots, and with his ute's tray piled with shovels, rakes, hessian bags, a petrol water pump, and other fire fighting gear.

When Libby ran out to meet him, he said without preamble, 'I don't think the fire will get this far, but you can head to my place after we're finished here, just in case.'

'Me?' She frowned up at him. 'What about you?'

'I'll head to Reg's farm, lend a hand with fightin' the blaze.'

With hands on hips she stared into his face and said flatly, 'Not on your own, you're not.'

He paused to eye her before saying, 'You'd be safer at my place.'

'And so would you. But you're not going there, are you.' It was a statement, not a question.

He gave a half smile and shook his head at her. 'Right-oh. Where d'you wanna start?'

'Let's move the stock to the furthest paddock, make sure all the troughs are full, and then we'll....'

Late that night they sat in soot-covered overalls on Libby's veranda, cold stubbies of beer in their hands. The only clean-ish spots on her face were around her eyes and mouth, and when she freed her ash-greyed hair from the tight ponytail, it bounced up and out like a gritty Afro.

Sitting beside her, long legs stretched out front, MJ gave a bark of laughter and his teeth flashed white against his grimy face. 'You look like one of those famous minstrels.'

'You can talk,' she jibed. 'Checked the mirror lately?'

Still chuckling, he swallowed a mouthful of beer and gave a long, satisfied, 'Ahhh.'

Beside him, Libby smiled. 'You said it.'

He flicked her a glance. 'Say, I didn't think you were a drinker, Lib?'

'I'm not ... normally. Dad left these beers here and I'm glad he did, 'cos they're doing a fine job of washing the ashes down my throat.' Turning her sooty, minstrel-like face to grin at him, she raised her stubby in a toast. 'Here's to Dad.'

'And to members of the rural fire service,' MJ added.

'Yes, them too.'

After clinking stubbies they sat in companionable silence, drinking beer and watching the red glow from the bushfire slowly diminish before disappearing entirely.

2

'Oh no.' Running an anxious hand down the gelding's nearside foreleg, Libby sucked in a breath and dropped to her haunches. 'Shorty's hurt.'

From inside the horse truck a deep voice called, 'What?' and a moment later a rangy, well muscled man appeared, leading a bay mare down the ramp. The spirited bay tossed her head and danced when her black hooves touched the sparsely grassed ground. The man let her prance briefly, and then reined her in to come alongside Libby and the liver chestnut gelding.

'I should've bandaged his legs, MJ.' She looked up at him, her hazel eyes troubled, and raised a hand. The tips of her long, slender fingers were crimson with blood. 'But he normally floats so well.' At a chime from her pocket she clicked her tongue and rose, wiped her hand on her jeans leg, and tugged out her mobile to check the caller ID. 'Damn. I should take this. It's Dad.'

'Go ahead.' MJ passed her the mare's lead rope. 'I'll take care of Shorty.'

Murmuring, 'Thanks,' she watched him take his familiar 'thinking' stance to quietly survey the gelding.

She'd once asked him why he liked to stand that way, with his long legs apart and hands tucked into the back of his pants. After eyeing her for a thoughtful moment he'd drawled, 'What else is a man 'sposed to do with his arms when he's just standin' around, thinkin'?'

It was the first time he'd referred to himself as a man, at least when talking to her, but she gave it no mind. He was merely her childhood friend, familiar as the native paddock grasses that grew green and supple under the winter rains, to become tawny and resilient in the dry heat of summer.

When he squatted to run confident exploratory hands from the horse's nearside fetlock to the coronet, Libby accepted the call. 'Hi Dad. Thanks for ringing back, but it's all sorted.'

After gently thumbing aside the blood-matted hair to inspect the oozing laceration, MJ carefully set the leg back down.

'So you got to the marathon okay?' At the boom of Dave Barnes' voice across the phone connection, Libby held the mobile out from her ear and moved a short distance away. The mare followed, happy to pick at a new patch of grass.

'MJ was able to bring us in his truck. While my float sits idle at home, thanks to that damn ute of mine.'

Her father's exasperated breath whooshed from the speaker. 'I hope you'll finally replace that rust-bucket this year. It's letting you down too often—makes us worry every time you take it on a long trip.'

'You and me both.' Libby's eyes followed MJ as he circled the gelding, checking for other injuries. 'I've been wanting to replace the ute for years,' she went on distractedly. 'Yet here I am, still having to rely on others for transport.'

'I'm sure MJ doesn't mind helpin' out. He's a top lad.'

Turning her head away, she brought the phone close to her mouth. 'Don't start.'

'Just sayin' it's lucky MJ is around to pitch in while you've got no man on your side of the fence to ... well ... share the load, so to speak.'

Again with the old 'a woman on her own MUST be doing it tough' assumption.

Et tu, Dad?

'Yeah, well things are just fine the way they are on my "side of the fence".' She swept a strand of sun-bronzed brunette hair out of her eyes with a work-toned upper arm. 'You're right about the ute, though. Sticky-taping the rust-bucket won't work for much longer, but for now every cent has to go into the farm.'

'Mmm. I know what that's like.' After a thoughtful pause Dave said slowly, 'Your mother and I could ... help with some funds?' Hearing Libby's intake of breath, he rushed on. 'Make that we'd *like* to help, not to mention ease our minds knowing you had a reliable vehicle.'

'And I appreciate the offer, Dad, but you and Mum are self-funded retirees now and don't have spare cash to splash around.'

'We wouldn't consider helping our only child to be "splashing cash"—'

'I know, but what reserves you have now will need to last the distance. And you should be spending some on enjoying your retirement ... doing those things you couldn't when the two of you were tied to the property.'

When behind her MJ muttered, 'Need to grab a dressing,' she turned with a worried frown and watched him head inside the truck. 'Remember when we first discussed my taking over the farm, Dad? How the three of us agreed I would do it on my own?'

Boronia Station, named for the sweet-smelling wildflowers that grew in every uncleared pocket on the cattle property, had been in the Barnes family for generations, passed from father to son in the long-held farming tradition. As it had with his forebears, the station's dust coursed through Dave's veins. This meant selling was not an option, even when his wife's medical needs necessitated a move to Perth.

While the only other option was to hand over the property to their daughter—their son having died in infancy, a pain Dave would take to his grave—it was also a break from tradition that set bushy grey eyebrows twitching in the local farming community.

Although he didn't say as much, Libby knew her father sorely missed working the farm. At least their new home in a retirement village on Perth's south coast, paid for out of the financial settlement they'd all agreed upon for transfer of the farm—a mere pittance compared to the property's market value—was less than two hundred kilometres away. This allowed them to visit often, and meant Dave could lend a hand at musters and other busy times. And he stayed in regular touch by phone, always ready to provide valuable advice.

Advice she was drawing upon less and less lately; something he acknowledged with a mixture of pride and regret.

'Sure I do, but ... we could treat it like a loan, keep it just between ourselves—'

'Da-ad.' A head shake accompanied the drawn-out word. 'You know what this close-knit community is like, how everyone knows everything about everyone else. Those bored old cow cocky retirees who've been sitting around just waiting for the chance to say, "Told'ya it was a bad idea handin' over the farm to a girl," are still watching and waiting. If word got out I'd accepted money from you, whether as a loan or otherwise, they'd be rubbing their idle hands in glee and heading straight to the pub to broadcast the news.'

'And what do you reckon the townsfolk would think of

your mother and me, if they knew you'd borrowed *more* high-interest money from the bank when we could've helped you out financially?' When she didn't respond, her father sighed. 'I do understand, Lib. You need to prove yourself to the doubters.'

'Yes, I do.'

'Just remember ... the offer's there if ever you need it.'

'Thanks, Dad. I'll remember.'

'And we have every confidence in you, my girl. Wouldn't have trusted you with the farm if we didn't.'

She smiled at the ground and scuffed the dirt with the toe of a riding boot. 'That means a lot.' Then she noticed MJ emerge from the truck's interior carrying a bottle of blue antiseptic lotion and a rolled bandage, and her smile wilted. She watched him drop to his haunches beside the gelding and begin gently applying lotion to the injured area, murmuring soothing words as he dressed the wound.

'You still there, Lib?'

'Yeah, sorry. Look, I'd better go. The marathon will be kicking off soon.'

'Right-oh. Well, show 'em your heels.'

'Will let you know how we go. Love to you and Mum.'

As she ended the call, MJ squinted up at her. 'Did you tell him about Shorty?'

She shook her head. 'Couldn't face giving them more bad news. That's all I ever seem to have for them since taking over the farm.'

'Well, Dave and Rhonda know bad news comes with

the territory.' MJ rubbed his now purple-stained hands down the legs of his jeans. The bright colour had seeped into the scars, nicks, and creases in the skin, making his hands look like marked-up roadmaps.

'Yep, Dad's nothing if not a realist.'

'And a top bloke.'

'Mmm.' She watched MJ unroll the bandage, and mused on the high regard the two men had for each other.

It wasn't simply because they'd been neighbouring graziers. A grateful MJ credited his farming successes to Dave's mentorship in the early years, after Bob Johnson died in a tractor accident and left MJ and his widowed mother to run the farm on their own.

Despite having never enjoyed living on the land, Yvonne Johnson couldn't bear to sell the farm, the place her husband had called his 'Shangri-La', so she passed it to their son and moved to Perth to be closer to her siblings.

Libby too had received the benefit of her father's wisdom gleaned over sixty years working the land. But as a single young woman managing a cattle property alone, she had something MJ didn't—the eyes and ears of the community focused on her, waiting for the 'inevitable' slip-up....

MJ began wrapping the bandage around the gelding's injury. 'So, that ute of yours.'

'What about it?'

'Seems to me it might be on the verge of breathing its last. Then what'll you do for transport?'

'Don't know. It's not like I have other options ... apart from making the Fergie my daily drive,' she said drily. 'Only she's not in the best condition either, as you know.'

MJ's chocolate brown eyes crinkled at the corners and a grin tugged at his lips. 'Can picture you roarin' into town on that old Ferguson tractor, dressed to the nines for one of them high teas ... or whatever they're called.'

'Oh, very funny. I'll have you know I've been to *one* high tea in my whole life, and it was a hospital fundraiser. And speaking of hospitals....' Bending, she eyed the gelding's leg. 'How bad is it?'

'Reckon he scraped the skin off with his rear hoof.' MJ tilted his square, slightly prominent chin at the laceration site. 'This is the only spot that needs a dressing, though both back legs have hair scraped off 'em too.' As he spoke, he finished applying and tying off the bandage. 'Poor bugger must've lost his footing and slid forward on his hocks when I swerved to avoid that semi-trailer on the way here.' He sat back on his heels and flicked her an apologetic glance. 'Real sorry 'bout that, Lib.'

'Wasn't your fault. That semi driver strayed into our lane. If you hadn't swerved, we wouldn't be here talking about it.'

Lowering his eyes, he dragged tense fingers through his black-brown fringe in a familiar gesture. 'Shorty'll probably favour that leg for a while. And even if he's not limping, I doubt the course vet will allow him to compete with such a fresh injury.'

She winced into his longish face. 'My team's gonna be devastated, damn it. They've been working so hard in the lead-up....'

He stared back at her, one hand rasping over the dark stubble on his chin. Then his gaze slid to the horse at her side.

The mare stood with her pretty head bent, sniffing the crushed grass around her.

Dusting off his hands, MJ got to his feet. 'You could use Red instead.'

Libby's mouth dropped open. 'You'd let me ride her in the event?' She eyed the bright red bay. 'But you only brought her along to get more experience with being transported and attending events.'

'She's fit enough to compete, I've been workin' her hard lately.' When he stepped in to run a hand down her satiny neck, pausing to finger the 'prophet's thumbprint', a small depression in the muscle below her crest, the mare tossed her head as if nodding agreement. 'She's young but learning fast. And competing here would be good practice for the Quilty.'

'So you're serious about entering the Tom Quilty this year?'

'A national endurance riding championship being held in our area for the first and possibly last time? It's just too good an opportunity to miss. And it'd be fitting if a local was to win.'

'Completing a hundred miles in twenty-four hours is a big ask for a young horse.'

'The distance shouldn't faze her, but I'll have to start monitoring our ride times. The race is still months away, so we don't have to rush our preparation.' Upward creases formed in the corners of his firm mouth. 'Reckon that Tom Quilty gold cup'll be bonza on my mantelpiece.'

'Bonza also having your name and Red's go down in Australian history as a champion combination of horse and rider.'

'Yep.'

Libby frowned. 'So ... you wouldn't want anything bad to happen to her in the lead-up—'

'She'll be in safe hands today. Nothing bad will happen.'

'You can't know that. This twisty, obstacle-peppered course has claimed competitors in the past—'

'Yeah, mostly inattentive, gung-ho riders, or youngsters on ill-prepared mounts. You're none of those things, and neither is Red. She's fresh and still a bit flighty, but nothing you can't handle.'

Libby stared at him, doubt shining in her thickly lashed eyes.

Cherry Red was his pride and joy, the best so far produced from his careful breeding programme using Australian Stockhorse champion sire, Red Letter. With a sweet-natured thoroughbred dam of flawless conformation, and a good dose of Arab in her sire's bloodline, Red would come close to claiming the Anglo/Arab breeding preferred by the majority of endurance riders.

If something happened to the spirited mare during the nineteen kilometre ride, would Libby be able to live with herself?

The fourth leg of the quintathlon, the horse ride followed on from a ten kilometre foot race, an eight kilometre canoe sprint, and a one kilometre swim of the chilly Arthur River. The final stage of the relay, a twenty kilometre cycle race, finished at the historic Moodee Community Hall on the banks of the river.

From where it sat, aged but steadfast amid a stand of majestic red gums, the timber hall easily accommodated the competitors and crowds of spectators who gathered to watch the teams compete.

People came from all over to attend the event, held annually in the state's picturesque lower south. Many now perched on the hall's thick-cut timber stairs waiting for the event to kick off, partaking of the hot drinks offered by a posse of volunteers, and tossing muffin crumbs to a family of keen-eyed magpies.

With almost forty teams registered to compete, this year's 'Moodee' was predicted to be the most exciting yet.

Standing silently chewing her lip, Libby ran her eyes over the assembled trucks and floats, all with horses tethered to them. Some stood calmly dozing, while others pawed and snorted as their riders and strappers buzzed around, preparing them for what would prove a gruelling course for some, and a warm-up for the forthcoming Blackwood Marathon for others.

At the sound of booted footfalls she turned to see MJ once more stride up the non-slip ramp into the truck. His short-sleeved checked shirt could've used a press but was clean, judging by the whiffs of washing powder fragrance she'd caught while seated in the cab next to him. His jeans probably were too, despite the blue lotion stains and neatsfoot oil marks on the butt and inside legs—marks that made her smile, knowing they came from time spent in the saddle.

MJ did alright for a farming bloke living alone, and she was lucky to have him to call on in times of need. It went both ways, with him occasionally calling on her to lend a hand, like in haying season. He'd get her to take the wheel of the tractor hauling the baler, while he hoisted the finished bales on the following truck. And the time he gashed his leg with the chainsaw she'd been over there in a flash, to step into the role of nurse and emergency farmhand.

In times of need it was just what neighbouring farmers did.

When Red shifted beside her to paw the ground, Libby put a hand on her twitching neck and murmured low, soothing words. She could feel the strong muscles beneath the satiny bay coat.

The horse *was* in brilliant condition, and accepting MJ's

offer *would* save her team from having to forfeit and wait a whole 'nother year to try again ... no doubt with someone different to do the ride. But using an unfamiliar horse in the race was risky, even more so when that horse was scheduled to compete in a national championship event in the near future.

'Glad I brought her along today.' MJ's voice issued from the truck's front storage area. Moments later he emerged with a well-used, well-oiled snaffle bridle dangling from one tanned arm, and a stock saddle and cloth slung over the other.

'Are you sure? I mean, *really* sure you want to risk it?'

Fixing her with a level gaze he held out the bridle, and when she continued frowning uncertainly at him, gave it a jiggle. 'Use my gear. It's sized for Red, so won't need any adjustment.'

With a hesitant, 'I don't know about this....' she extended a hand, and he pushed the bridle into it.

'Come on, shake a leg.' He gave a wry huff. 'My mates'd never let me forget it if my purpose-bred mare ran last.'

3

The dappled grey tossed its head when the man made to slip the bridle over its swivelling, black-tipped ears. Muttering curses, he yanked on the halter rope to bring the horse's head down.

'That thing even broken?' Another, taller man in a camel-coloured felt Akubra hat, checked western shirt, and cream moleskins above patterned cowboy boots, emerged from behind the horse truck to eye the performance.

'She'll be alright,' the strapper said gruffly. 'Just head shy 'n a bit fresh is all. Hold her in check for the first few Ks, she should settle after that.'

The tall rider scowled as the rangy grey pulled away again to dance at the end of the reins, sending the unfastened throatlatch into crazed mid-air figure eights.

When the buckle whacked it on the cheek, the horse gave a startled grunt and tossed its wild-eyed head.

'You do realise,' the rider went on smoothly, 'I entered this event to *win,* not to end up on my arse in the dirt.'

'Oh yeah,' the strapper puffed as he struggled to calm the over-excited animal, 'I was forgettin' how much winning means to you.' Throwing the rider a sarcastic glance, he shoved the reins into his hands. 'For now, champ, make yourself useful and hold 'er while I get the saddle on. And buckle that damn strap. Once you're on board I'll lead you to the marshalling area.'

'You're gonna *lead* me over there? What am I, a child on his first pony ride?'

'Look, if you'd prefer to be tossed the instant your butt hits the saddle...?'

'I'll get on here and settle her, then ride over there on my own.'

'Well, alrightee then. What do I know, anyway? I only *own* the horse.' The caustic comment earned the strapper a narrow-eyed glower.

The grey sky hung heavy overhead but so far the rain had held off. Libby stood holding Red's reins, scuffing her riding boots in the sandy soil, chewing her lip, and *burning* to get going. She glanced down the line of waiting riders in the marshalling area. Tightly bunched, they looked similarly keyed-up after the pre-ride briefing. At least Red appeared unaffected, standing quietly at her side, ears flicking to and fro with casual interest.

This waiting is torture.

As she thought that, a surge of watery activity from the nearby river had her snapping to attention. Seeing the second batch of dripping swimmers scrambling up the riverbank, she swept a searching gaze over them and glimpsed a recognisable figure.

Jamie!

Adrenaline flared and she thrust an arm in the air to get his attention. As soon as he was making for them at a soggy lope, she leaned forward and extended a hand, taking care to keep her feet behind the marshalling line.

After trotting up to her grinning and dripping river water, he gave her hand a rushed, wet slap and puffed, 'We're in the top ten. Go!' He watched her flick the reins over Red's head and swing into the saddle, before hurrying to join his teammates and take the proffered towel.

From where he stood amid the throng of spectators, MJ watched the mare spring into a spirited canter even before Libby's right foot was in the stirrup. Moments later they disappeared from sight.

Beside him, a sniffing Jamie towelled his hair. 'Wow, that was intense. So, how d'ya reckon she'll go in the ride?'

'Alright.'

'What's the course like?'

'Long. Nineteen Ks.' MJ thought back to the pre-ride briefing he'd gone along to with Libby. The course official had shown the competitors a rough map of the route and outlined the usual information on track markers and checkpoints, hazards, and vetting procedures. 'Cuts through surrounding properties so there'll be tight turns, gateways, and a few obstacles, but nothin' they can't handle.'

'Well signposted?'

'Apparently.'

'Sounds easy enough, unlike the swim. Man, that was like being in a food processor! People chopping up the water all around, some even swimming right over you.'

Thinking that a nineteen kilometre, obstacle-laden horse ride couldn't really be compared to a one kilometre swim for degree of difficulty, MJ gave a noncommittal grunt and moved off.

For the first kilometre the fresh, now excited mare fought for her head, before settling into a smooth, ground-eating canter that allowed Libby to relax in the saddle. First impressions of the horse? MJ was right, Red was a promising Quilty prospect.

A ground-level flag fluttered in the breeze ahead of them, and Libby brought an image of the course map to front of mind. Yep, they were coming to the second tight turn and a two-gates crossing.

When hooves thundered up behind them, Red tossed her head and quickened her pace. Libby shortened the reins, holding the mare in check, as a dappled grey raced past them, sending grassy clods flying.

Slow down, idiot, or you're never gonna make the turn.

As if reading her thoughts, the grey's rider hauled on the reins. When his horse responded by opening its mouth and throwing up its head, the man yanked harder on the left rein in a vain attempt to make the turn. The grey lurched, slid sideways, and plaited its legs.

Libby winced at the glimpse of sky between the man's moleskinned butt and the saddle. Then his feet flew up and out of the stirrups and he was off, pitching toward the ground. His mount, after stumbling to the side, recovered its balance and took off with a flash of pigrooting hooves and spray of clods.

With a quick glance behind at the trailing field, Libby reined in beside the fallen rider. 'You okay?'

He sat up, grimacing and rubbing his back. 'I'll live.' He had a deep, smoky voice, and met her gaze with a pair of piercing blue eyes below dark, downward-slanting eyebrows. Fashionable stubble underlined his straight nose and shaded his square jawline.

While he might be a careless rider, the 'idiot' was also a handsome sod.

Libby's heart banged against her rib cage, catching her by surprise. Releasing her sucked-in breath, she said, 'Your horse is heading for the hills.'

He glanced to where the grey was disappearing over a rise with a toss of its head. 'Yeah.'

'You gonna be alright to get back?'

With a nod, he rose to his feet, brushing off his grass-stained pants. 'Yep.'

The idiot was tall too, and well built.

'Right-oh.' At the sounds of horses approaching from behind, she said hurriedly, 'I'll leave you to it.'

'Thanks for stopping.' His teeth were eye-catchingly white in his tanned face.

Dipping her head at him, Libby wheeled Red and headed for the gateway. Once through it she let the mare stretch out and gain speed, only reining her back to an easy canter once they'd passed the next group of riders.

At this rate we'll at least stay in the top ten.

A short distance on they turned past a pocket of trees and Libby felt the mare twitch beneath her.

Something was wrong.

And that something was straight ahead, close beside their path.

A windmill, and a working one at that. Its metal wheel spun in the breeze overhead and its rust-red corrugated iron tail fin rotated in the swirling gusts.

It had been among the obstacles the course official mentioned in the briefing. Although he'd warned the riders they'd need to pass close by it, Libby hadn't thought much of it at the time. Shorty didn't bother about things like windmills.

But I'm not on Shorty now. Has Red been near a mill before, or even seen one working? If not, this could be interesting.

As they drew nearer the looming 'monster' and Red tensed beneath her, Libby peered up at the mill. After decades of operation, its ageing metallic parts rattled, creaked, and groaned as together they brought the precious bore water to the surface. The sounds, combined with its height and unpredictable movements, made the windmill a scary contraption for a young horse to confront for the first time.

Red flicked one ear back at Libby's soothing, 'Easy, girl,' but swiftly brought it forward again to focus on the ogre in front of them.

Oblivious to the impact of its intimidating presence, the mill continued grinding and whirring as it spewed water into the nearby tank and attached livestock trough.

Knowing it would only upset Red further if she tried to push her past the obstacle, Libby let the mare slow her pace until they were almost jogging on the spot. While anxiously waiting for Red to settle, Libby glimpsed movement on the ground nearby.

The lone magpie looked up from its foraging to meet her gaze, until another sound had it returning to the safety of the leafy undergrowth. Libby too was alerted by the sound, and risked a peek over her shoulder.

The group of riders they'd passed earlier was swiftly catching up to them.

Leaning forward, she said calmly to Red's flicking ears, 'Well, girl, you have a choice to make. Either brave the windmill or let those riders we passed before overtake us.'

As if understanding the words Red's twitching muscles compressed like springs beneath the saddle, and her hooves danced in frustrated motion.

The approaching riders were almost upon them.

With a sudden thrust from her hindquarters that almost unseated Libby, Red leapt into a standing gallop, dropping her head defensively as they passed the monster's whirling wheel.

Libby clung on and let the mare run for a bit, then gradually brought her back to a controlled canter as the group behind them dropped out of sight.

Whew, major obstacle overcome.

Further along they crossed a shallow creek, hurdled a fallen tree in a gateway, and passed barking dogs and yahooing children at a farmhouse, all without pause. And then they rounded a bend and there it was.

The finish line.

An avenue of spectators had gathered there to greet every finishing rider, while on the other side of the line, cyclists stood beside their bikes anxiously waiting to be tagged. Theirs was the final, crucial leg, when race leaders could be reeled in and overtaken by underdogs.

As the closest spectators spotted her and began waving and cheering, pride and gratitude rose to fill Libby's chest and throat. She bent to give Red's sweaty neck a congratulatory pat, murmuring to the twitching ears, 'We made it, girl. Well done.'

Once they'd loped across the finish line and tagged their eager cyclist, she slowed the mare to a walk.

Just one final obstacle to go, the vet check. Though if MJ was right, Red should have no trouble passing it.

The man himself, peeling away from where he'd been standing with the crowd, strode up to walk beside them. At his drawled, 'You must've overtaken a few,' she asked, 'Where did we finish?'

'Seventh.'

'I was hoping we'd picked up more places than that, but I guess three's better than nothing.'

'Yep, 'specially with competition this intense. Want a water?'

'Oh, yes please.'

Once they were at the truck, MJ grabbed a bottle of water from inside the cab while she dismounted.

At the question in his eyes she rasped through dry lips, 'Red was brilliant, but I'll tell you later about the windmill.'

His brow creased and he opened his mouth, until she raised a hand and croaked, 'Later.' Putting the bottle to her lips she took a long drink, splashed some water on her dusty face and wiped her forearm across it, and cleared her throat. 'Now I'd better head to the vetting area.'

'Right-oh.'

As she led Red toward the waiting vet, Libby spotted the 'handsome idiot' sitting in a deck chair beside another horse truck, swigging a can of beer. Seeing her, he flashed a smile and raised the can in a salute. There was no sign of the dappled grey, and she wondered idly if he'd even bothered to go after the horse.

Murmuring, 'She's in brilliant condition,' the vet withdrew the stethoscope and smiled at Libby. 'That's a good, strong heartbeat and she's recovered well. You've done a great job with her preparation.'

'Not me,' Libby replied, running a hand down the mare's face. 'I only rode her.' She lifted a chin over her shoulder to indicate the waiting MJ. 'That's her breeder and trainer, the tall bloke sitting on the truck's ramp over there.'

The vet flicked him a glance. 'Well, he's done a fine job.'

'I'll pass that on.'

4

While MJ finished rubbing down and settling Red for the night, Libby freshened up in the hall's amenities. Changed into jeans and white slim-line tunic, her long hair brushed back into what might qualify as a loose French twist, she added a dash of lipstick and, satisfied with her appearance, strolled to the hall on her own.

With country music blaring from inside it, bonfires blazing from forty-four gallon drums outside it, and party lights and Chinese lanterns lighting its interior, the hall was ready for the traditional post-race shindig. Despite the early hour, the crowd was already letting their hair down, drinking, eating barbecued steak burgers and hot chips, laughing, celebrating, commiserating, and dancing.

'There you are.'

Whirling around, Libby found the handsome 'idiot' smiling down at her and holding out a can of beer.

'Been watching for you.'

'Oh?'

'Wanted to shout you a drink, to thank you for stopping to check on me.' As he spoke, he held out the dripping can. 'Name's Cal. Short for Callum.'

'Well ... that's nice of you, Cal, but not necessary. I was only doing what anyone would've done.'

'But nobody else did. They all just sped on past.' He waved the can at her. 'C'mon, don't leave me hangin'.'

The crease deepened between her sweeping brows as she accepted the ice-cold can. 'Thanks.' She shook the condensation off her hands. 'I'll give it to my friend.'

'You're not a beer drinker?'

'Not much of a drinker at all.' The warmth in his gaze made her fidget. 'And if I do have a drink, it's usually wine. But—'

'Right then, wine it is.' Spinning on his cowboy-booted heels, he made for the bar area.

'Who was that?'

Libby gave a start as MJ came to stand beside her. 'Just another competitor. Says his name's Cal. He had a fall at one of the gates and I stopped to check he was okay. Apparently he feels obliged to buy me a drink as a thank-you.' She held out the beer can. 'This was his first attempt. Enjoy.'

'First attempt?'

'Seems he's determined to get me something I'll actually drink.'

Peering at the queue jostling in front of the bar, MJ caught the man in question gazing back at Libby with an expression he recognised. Muttering, 'And that's not all he's determined to get,' he clicked the can open and raised it to his lips.

'What?'

'Nothin'. Say, I've been practising my dance moves.'

'Oh yeah?'

'So what about you and me—'

'Gidday, mate.' Striding up to them, wine glass in one hand and icy stubby in the other, Cal flashed a questioning grin at a poker-faced MJ.

Holding the other man's gaze, MJ dipped his head while beside him Libby said, 'Cal, this is MJ.'

'Ah.' Cal glanced at Libby's unadorned ring finger. 'Husband?'

She gave a smiling shake of her head.

'Boyfriend then?'

Another head shake. 'Friend and neighbour. Saved the day by giving me a lift here.'

'Do I take it you don't have either? Husband or boyfriend?'

Gazing levelly at him, she said slowly, 'Neither.'

'Well then.' Cal's grin broadened and he stared into her eyes. 'That makes this a good news day.'

Libby coloured and lowered her gaze, while MJ turned away to drain his beer.

When the band struck up with the Dixie Chicks' song *Cowboy Take Me Away,* Cal set down his half-finished stubby. 'That's my cue.' Moving closer to gaze down at Libby, he extended a hand. 'May I have this dance?'

'I ... well....' Dithering, Libby looked to MJ but he was making for the bar, tossing his empty beer can in the recycling bin on the way. Turning back, she met Cal's charismatic, self-assured smile.

He waved his extended hand at her. 'Don't leave me hanging here. C'mon. This is a top song to dance to.'

'Yes, but—'

'You don't want to spend the whole evening standing around watching other people have all the fun, do you?'

'No, but—'

'Okay, then.' Taking the glass from her hand, he slipped a strong arm around her waist. With a chuckle rumbling in his throat he whisked her, laughing despite herself, onto the dance floor.

'The Fergie ended up in the shop for repairs right when I was due to cut the firebreaks. Luckily I was able to borrow MJ's gear to get them done.'

'That old tractor will have plenty more years in her yet.'

'Once she's fixed. Oh, and we've *finally* replaced that

last section of burnt fencing.'

'By "we" I take it you mean you and MJ?'

'Yep.' Libby frowned at her father's snippiness. He was obviously preparing to say something he knew would provoke a reaction.

'Glad you got that finished,' he went on. 'The temporary fence we set up wouldn't have withstood a shove from a determined beast. Boy, would I like to get my hands on whoever set the bush alight with that illegal still.'

'Yeah, well that doesn't seem likely after all this time. Though the Police do say their investigations are "ongoing". Anyway, we managed to scrounge most of the timber from the block, so the job didn't cost a bomb.'

Following a charged silence, Dave's sigh whooshed over the phone connection. 'You and MJ.'

Here it comes.

'Cal not around to pitch in?'

It was her turn to sigh. She and Cal had been together for months now, yet her parents still refused to accept him as a long term prospect.

'He was working.'

'He's always working, just not on the farm.'

'That's shift work for you, Dad. And these twenty-four hour shifts at the mine are real style crampers.' She heard herself repeating Cal's own words, only she couldn't punctuate the statement with the winning smiles and apologetic cuddles that always won her over. She blew a long breath.

'Yet he somehow manages to get to the pub for all the darts and Texas Hold'em comps,' Dave muttered darkly.

'Da-ad.'

'I know, I know. But it has to be said—'

'No, it doesn't.'

'Yes, it does, and this isn't only me talking. Your mother feels the same.' He took a deep breath. 'We're ... happy ... you're not on your own anymore, even though we'd always hoped—'

'I know what you hoped.' A sarcastic edge crept into her voice. 'Which of course had *nothing* at all to do with the fiscal advantages of amalgamating our two properties.'

Her father's tone grew defensive. 'That's not the only reason it'd be a good match, but it's a benefit that can't be overlooked or overstated. And land—'

'Is a farmer's most precious commodity, I know. You've drummed that into me from childhood.'

'It was an important lesson, one everyone has to learn if they're to make a go of working on the land.'

'Yeah—'

'And at the risk of repeating myself, that's not the only reason we hoped you and MJ would get together.' Dave gave an affronted sniff. 'You know each other so well ... been friends since you were kids.'

'Friends, yes. But the thought of us "getting it on" for the sake of convenience makes me queasy.'

'I never said—'

'MJ is ... so different to Cal, love,' Rhonda called from

the background, her voice husky. 'I don't mean simply looks-wise, although he has a rugged charm that makes him a good sort in his own way. And to my eyes, a better sort.' Her voice grew strained. 'Pass me the phone, Dave.' She gave a small, dry cough. 'He might be a man of few words, but what's inside is more important than the "gift of the gab", or external appearances. And while he may not be as handsome or eloquent as Cal, MJ is trustworthy, loyal, considerate, and dependable.'

'I know all this, Mum. And you sound a bit ... croaky ... this morning.'

'Don't fuss. I simply haven't got 'round to using my puffer yet.' Her tone softened. 'Sorry for snapping at you, love. It's just ... I'm still coming to terms with this damn asthma. As if one chronic ailment wasn't enough....'

'No need to apologise, Mum, I understand. And I worry about you.'

'Thanks, love, but I don't want you worrying. I'm just having a bad day.' Rhonda cleared her throat. 'Now, getting back to what I was saying ... I can't help wondering if maybe you never got around to seeing MJ as anything other than the boy next door. And now you've been swept away by Cal's looks and charm.'

Libby frowned. 'You're both talking as if MJ wants more from our relationship, but what gives you that idea? I know him better than you do, and I reckon he's like me, perfectly happy with our friendship as it stands.'

After a pause, Rhonda said, 'Remember when he asked

you to the end-of-year school formal after you'd both finished senior?'

Libby winced. 'Why bring that up after all this time?'

'Because I think his confidence took a hard knock that day. After all, you had agreed to go to the formal with him but at the eleventh hour ditched him for that other boy ... was his name Aaron?'

'Yes, and thanks for reminding me what a little so-'n-so I was back then. In my defence, I'd had the hots for Aaron all my secondary school years, and I wasn't alone. He was such a hunk, every second girl in school felt the same. I'd given up hoping he'd one day look twice at me, and then his invitation came out of the blue. It was an opportunity I simply couldn't miss, and I really didn't think MJ would care. He and I were school buddies, always playing around, never serious about anything.'

'Of course, you were only kids. But it struck me how much trouble he'd gone to at the time. Fronting up to the door in his Sunday best, holding a bouquet I reckon his mum picked for him from her flower garden, and looking so hopeful....'

'Ouch.' Libby squeezed her eyes shut and rubbed her temples hard, as if to remove the mental picture.

'Yes, and if you ask me,' her mother went on, 'he was trying to impress you, to make you see him as something more than simply a school buddy.'

'And while you were dilly-dallying with Mr Hot Stuff Aaron,' Dave cut in, taking the receiver back while Rhonda coughed behind him, 'Meghan got her mitts onto MJ. Only to later drop him like a hot rock when things started getting serious, or "real" like you youngsters say. I'm bettin' she couldn't face life as a farmer's wife and all the work that entails. A right little princess, that one.'

Libby could feel his condemnatory head shake across the phone line.

''Course that's all history now,' he went on. 'And on the subject of history ... even while you were both still teenagers I suspected MJ of carrying a torch for you, Lib.' Dave gave a proud sniff. 'And why wouldn't he? You'd grown into a real looker by then, havin' taken after your mum. Still, I didn't expect him to confess it to me, man to man, him being of few words 'n all. So it came as something of a surprise years later, on the night he won the darts comp and everyone was shouting him beers—'

'I remember that night. He got tipsy, which tends to happen when you drink too much.' Libby heard in the background her mother's puffer delivering a dose of airway-opening bronchodilator. 'It also tends to loosen tongues and make people say things they don't mean.'

'Yeah, he did get chatty but real serious-like, and I reckon he meant what he said.' Dave paused briefly. 'Now ... how did he put it? Oh yeah, "Dave, I have feelings for your daughter," just straight out like that.' There was a fond smile in Dave's voice as he recalled the scene. 'And as you're my only daughter....' Greeted with a tense silence, he went on gruffly, 'Anyway, there's your evidence, in MJ's own words. The silly bugger just took too long telling *you* how he felt.'

'Still a bit gun-shy after those earlier failures, perhaps,' Rhonda called from behind him. 'That thing with Meghan left him pretty cut-up. Remember how, before things went pear-shaped, he came over to ask my opinion on jewellery, wanting to know if it was true that women prefer diamonds over every other gem?'

She gave a tinkling laugh. 'I was a bit taken aback by the question, it was so out of character for him. Anyway, he eventually came clean and showed me a picture he'd torn from a magazine, of a dainty solitaire in a rose gold setting. I told him I thought any girl would be thrilled to be given a ring like that. And it would've suited Meghan perfectly ... although I didn't tell *him* that.' Rhonda blew a sympathetic breath. 'Such a petite, pretty girl. It's a shame she wasn't the marrying kind.'

'And while MJ was dilly-dallying over Miss Petite,' Dave went on brusquely, '"Shallow Cal" muscled in with our Lib.'

Rhonda's tongue-clicking and resigned, 'Oh, Dave,' was audible in the background.

'Don't call Cal that, Dad,' Libby interjected darkly.

'Just callin' a spade a spade.'

'And we all know what a spade's good for shovelling.'

'What did you just say to me, young lady?' her father barked.

'Sorry, Dad, but your meddling brings out the worst in me.'

'Meddling? We're only—'

'Trying to help, I know. But you're overlooking an important point.'

'Which is?'

'I love Cal, and he loves me.'

'I'm sure that's true, in your case at least. As far as Cal's feelings go, I have my doubts about a bloke who's real keen to move in with a girl but not so keen to propose to her.' He sniffed. 'MJ was prepared to do the right thing when Meghan suggested they shack up together. He proposed to her instead ... or would've done, if she'd stayed around instead of doin' a flit when she got wind of his intentions.'

'And look how that turned out for him. Oh come on, Dad. You're trying to apply old-fashioned rules in modern times, which is always a bad idea.'

'Humph.'

Libby charged on. 'Despite what you obviously think, ours isn't a flash in the pan relationship. Cal and I have a future together.' When her father's only response was a peeved huff, her voice grew steely. 'And as far as MJ is concerned, I always have and always will value him as a good friend and neighbour ... and that's all. So the subject is no longer up for discussion, okay?'

Another strained silence followed until Rhonda called, 'Of course, love,' while Dave muttered something unintelligible under his breath.

5

'What's up, babe?' Cal strode into the kitchen where she stood at the sink, head bent, staring into the detergent-frothed water.

Turning, she saw boot prints of caked mine mud leading from the front door. 'Cal, shoes!'

'Oh crap, I forgot again. Sorry.' Throwing her a wince, he tiptoed back to the door, dropping more dried mud along the way. While he proceeded to peel off his work wear, she grabbed a broom and dustpan and cleaned up the mess.

Once she'd finished, he pulled her in for a hug and dropped a kiss on her lips. Holding her at arm's length, he stared into her face. 'You were standing there looking all sad. What's up?'

'Nothing.'

He gazed into her eyes. 'Let me guess. You've been talkin' to your folks.'

'Um ... yes ... I was. And ... they're coming up on Saturday morning to spend the weekend with us.'

'Oh. Great.'

At the obvious lack of enthusiasm in his words, Libby gave his arm a conciliatory pat. 'They just need to get to know you better. Why don't you make an effort to spend as much time with them as possible this weekend? Pour on the charm and I'm sure they'll warm to you, like I did.' Smiling into his eyes she added coyly, 'Well, *sort of* like I did.'

He forced a responding smile, not letting on that he'd given up the charm offensive when for once it had failed him. It still irked him no end that despite his smiles and flattery, past beauty pageant winner Rhonda Barnes remained pleasant but cool toward him. And Dave Barnes, who was friendly and gregarious with *everyone*, was never anything but openly wary and tight-lipped with him.

Still, they didn't visit the farm all that often.

And with plenty of overtime on offer at the mine, a bloke could always make himself scarce when the need arose....

At the sound of a truck rumbling to a stop by the yards, Libby lifted her head. She and Rhonda were at the kitchen bench, dobbing Rhonda's homemade strawberry jam and whipped cream on a batch of freshly baked fruit scones.

From his seat at the table behind them, Dave looked up from his newspaper. 'Now who might that be?'

After a quick rinse of her hands, Libby strode to the door. 'Oh, it's Murray. With the load of hay I asked him to deliver *next week*. Damn.' She grimaced at her parents. 'He won't wait around or try again if I send him away, and I need the hay, my stocks are down to almost nothing. I'll have to unload it.'

Dave's chair scraped back from the table. 'Well then, let's get to it.'

'I'll take care of it, Dad, and seeing's how he's come early, Murray can pitch in. Won't take us long working together to unload it. You and Mum have some morning tea and a relax.'

Her father glared at her. 'If you think I'm gonna stay sitting on my behind while you're out there workin' yours off, you've got another think coming, my girl.'

'Dave—'

Stopping Rhonda's objection with a raised hand, he said gruffly, 'Hay might look light but the bales are heavy, especially after the first dozen or so. And Murray can be a lazy sod. Reckon you'll sling at least three to his one.' Dave pretended to sweep a glance around the room. 'And I don't see any other man here to lend a helping hand.'

Libby scowled at her father but had no comeback. There was no denying Cal was absent, having agreed to work the weekend shifts. And while he reasoned they needed the overtime money, she suspected that wasn't the only reason he'd chosen to spend most of this particular weekend at work. Then again, how could she blame him, considering her parents' attitudes toward him.

'What about MJ?' Rhonda asked. 'Maybe he'd pop over and give you a hand with the unloading?'

'No!' Blinking at the harshness of her response, Libby swallowed and went on more evenly. 'I don't want to bother him with something I can handle on my own.'

Stepping closer, Rhonda wrapped a warm hand around her daughter's arm and gazed knowingly into her eyes. 'You a bit ... uncomfortable around him, love?' she asked softly.

Libby's eyes clouded. 'Things are different between us lately, since ... well ... Cal. And after all your talk about us— MJ and me—I just ... feel different about him.'

Rhonda's brow creased. 'Oh love, we never meant to—' She was interrupted by the impatient blare of a truck's horn.

Libby dropped a quick peck on her mother's cheek. 'Don't wait for me, I'll have a cuppa when I'm done. Kettle's boiling, there's tea in the pot, and the cosy's in the bottom drawer. Oh, and keep an eye on the roast please Mum? The veges will need turning soon.'

Rhonda nodded, while Dave strode up behind them. 'No matter what either of you say,' he announced brusquely, 'I'm helping out, and that's that. And if he wants to be on his way sooner rather than later, Murray's gonna do his fair share too.'

She wouldn't say so, but after the first dozen or so bales had hit the floor of the hayshed, Libby was glad of her father's help. Despite the leather gloves she'd tugged on as they left the house, her hands throbbed and stung from grasping the twine bindings and then lifting and slinging the bales onto the already hay-strewn floor.

Her father had declined her offer of gloves, saying his hands were like chain-mail after years of working on the land. She hoped they still were as he puffed and grunted beside her, bending and heaving, bending and heaving.

Wishing she'd thought to grab broad-brimmed hats as well, she straightened and rested hands on hips, stretching her back and closing her eyes against the late morning glare. In a nearby gum tree, a magpie carolled sweetly while butcher birds circled the workers, dark eyes peeled for grasshoppers or other tasty insects taking flight amid the activity. The scent of dried grass filled the air, and clouds of hay dust and particles swirled and settled on every surface, most heavily on those slick with sweat.

Dave in particular was red-faced and perspiring, but like the other two, paused only briefly to cough when the dust filled his lungs. He had just slung a bale and grabbed another when he gave a louder, hacking cough. The bale slipped from his grasp, landing back on the truck's tray with a dull thump that made the other two glance over.

Seeing her father jerk upright, gasping and clutching his chest, Libby froze and the breath caught in her throat. And when his features twisted in shock and distress, she dropped the bale she was holding and rushed toward him, only to watch him take a stumbling step forward.

And collapse across the fallen bale.

'Lib!' Cal jogged up to where she sat, head back against the wall, staring at the waiting room ceiling.

Rhonda sat hunched in a chair, elbows on her knees and head in her hands, looking small beside her daughter.

'Oh, Cal.' Libby rose to meet him, fresh tears filling her eyes. 'You came. I wasn't sure....'

She collapsed into his open arms and he pulled her close. 'Sorry, babe. I was down in the pit so it took a while to get away.'

'You're here now,' she murmured thickly against his blue and yellow high-visibility shirt. 'That's all that matters.'

Holding her close, he rubbed her back and waited until she finally drew away before asking, 'How's Dave?'

She sniffed and raised her eyes, and he saw tears clinging to the long lashes. Swallowing, she said so quietly he had to bend his head to hear, 'S-suspected cardiac event.'

He passed her his handkerchief and glanced at Rhonda, who had roused herself and was watching them, worry deeply etched in every line of her face. Flashing her an encouraging smile, he turned back to Libby and murmured, 'Heart attack?'

She wiped her eyes. 'No details yet. They're still running tests.'

'Oh.' Cal looked at Rhonda again and was rewarded with a weak nod. 'Say, I'm overdue for a caffeine top-up,' he said brightly. 'What about you ladies? Fancy a coffee too?'

Flicking her silent, ashen-faced mother an anxious glance, Libby replied for them both. 'That'd be great, thanks.'

'Two flat whites?'

'Yes please. No sugar in either.'

'Got it. Back soon.' With a final squeeze of her arm, he strode off in search of the nearest coffee vending machine.

Libby watched him go, taking comfort from the confident strength radiating from his tall frame.

If only he'd been there when it happened....

The crease in the smooth skin between her brows deepened.

But would it have happened at all if he'd been there to help with the unloading?

6

'What the *hell* are you suggesting?' He glared at her from where he stood, spatula in hand, swathed in smoke rising from the sizzling barbeque plate.

Libby stared back at him with knitted brow, the bowl of tossed green salad in her hands forgotten for the moment.

In the days following the incident, she had tried not to brood over the reason her father had felt obliged to help with the hay unloading.

Tried, and failed.

She also tried to be tactful when broaching the subject with Cal, but he fired up the instant he realised what she was inferring.

Squinting accusingly at her through the aromatic steak-and-onions smoke, he barked, 'Are you really insinuating it's *my* fault your father collapsed while helping *you* unload some hay?'

At the reproach in his words her suppressed resentment flared, and she thumped the salad bowl onto the outdoor table, sending lettuce leaves jumping. 'Well you *never* seem to be around when there's work to be done on the farm, Cal. And because you'd decided working a weekend shift was preferable to spending time with my folks, Dad felt obliged to pitch in with the unloading.'

'Oh, come on—'

'No, *you* come on. We both know the real reason you accepted the "last minute" offer of overtime.'

Blowing through pursed lips, Cal turned his back to prod the cooking meat. 'You're jumping to conclusions again, Lib.'

'Am I? So tell me it's not true.'

He flipped the steaks, slapping them onto the hotplate and making them sizzle and spit. 'We've talked about this and I thought you understood.'

'So tell me again.'

'I'm working the extra overtime,' he said with a long-suffering sigh, 'because the farm can't support both of us *and* the bank loan.'

'It'd stand a better chance if you didn't spend so much money on ... non-essentials.'

'Non-essentials?' He bristled. 'Like what?'

'Like ... you somehow manage to never miss the darts comps or happy hours at the pub.'

'Can't a man spend a tiny fraction of his hard-earned wages on something he enjoys?'

'Hardly a "tiny fraction". You're there at least once every week.'

'Who's counting? Oh yeah, clearly *you* are.'

She went on as if he hadn't spoken. 'I didn't mind at first, until I realised it was a permanent arrangement.'

His expression darkened. 'You want me to stop spending time with my mates, is that it?'

'No, but why does it have to happen every single week? And why are you always shouting them beers when I've yet to see any of them return the favour?'

'So sue me for helping out some buddies who are doing it tough.'

'And *we're* not "doing it tough"?'

'Exactly why I'm working all this overtime.'

His attempt at a circular argument set her eyes rolling. 'Funny how these overtime shifts never impact your social life the way they do our family life.'

'*Your* family life.' His lips twisted. 'Dave and Rhonda are not *my* parents, thankfully.'

She rocked back on her heels to gape at him. Until that moment he'd never spoken to her like that, nor openly criticised her parents to her face. But that 'thankfully' was vicious. Still, there was no refuting the point he'd made. Dave and Rhonda *weren't* his parents, and considering Cal's attitude toward marriage, stood little chance of even becoming his in-laws.

Whenever the subject of marriage came up, which happened less and less of late, his standard response went along the lines of, 'People put so much importance on a scrap of paper, when all that really matters is how two people feel about each other.'

Even Beth, her favourite aunt and the family's unapologetic wedding junkie, had stopped asking when Libby's 'big day' might be happening.

Under her stunned, injured gaze, Cal's shoulders slumped and he dropped his chin to his chest. When he raised it again, regret had softened his expression. 'Sorry if I came across like a bastard just then, Lib.'

She continued staring into his handsome face as though trying to work out who he was.

'Don't know what came over me,' he went on. 'I didn't mean to bark at you like that.'

'But you *did* mean what you said, Cal.' Her voice, just above a whisper, held the threat of tears.

'Oh no, please don't cry.' Dropping the tongs on the side of the barbeque, he moved toward her and opened his arms. 'I can't bear to see you cry.'

She stiffened, but let him wrap her in a bear hug and stood breathing in the familiar scent of him, mostly heavy-duty pumice soap above mining machinery grease. To his dismay, and regardless of how often or carefully he showered, the mine worker smell appeared to have permanently attached itself to him.

'Y'gotta admit I was right though, babe,' he murmured above her head. 'They're not *my* parents, they're yours.'

'Of course I'm aware of that, I'm not *stupid*. But the way you—'

'Yeah, I shouldn't have spoken about your folks like that. They don't deserve it and neither do you.' When she remained silent, he held her at arms' length so he could look her in the eye. 'Come on, Lib, you know how I feel about family ... "stuff". It's important to you, which is totally fine. But after losing my mum at an early age and never even knowing who my father was, family just doesn't figure on my radar.'

'So I should stop trying to make it figure, is that what you're saying?'

'Go ahead and do what makes you happy is what I'm saying.' He pulled her close again. 'Just don't expect me to always be part of the happy families stuff, 'cos it's simply not my scene. And I'm real sorry about what happened to your dad but it was an accident, Lib. Accidents happen, especially on farms, and Dave knows that better than anyone.'

He was right, and she knew it.

No one was to blame for her father's heart condition. Dave himself said it could've been brought on by anything —an overly energetic game of golf, or even mowing the tiny patch of lawn behind their retirement village unit. Instead it happened on his beloved farm, while he was doing something worthwhile to help his equally beloved daughter. And the doctors said he'd be as good as new after the insertion of the cardiac stent, so what was all the fuss about?

Is Dad right, am I fussing too much?

And am I expecting too much of Cal? After all, he is working all this overtime for our joint benefit. And we haven't been together all that long, even though it feels like ... like....

As the thoughts tumbled over each other in her mind, the fight went out of her and she sagged against him.

Like I've loved Cal all my life....

Standing at the kitchen bench a few weeks later, humming as she beat the softened butter and sugar together, she pictured Cal's broad grin on arriving home from day shift to find a freshly baked carrot cake with cream cheese frosting waiting for him. It was his favourite sweet indulgence—next only to her he'd said more than once, earning himself a kiss, hug, or loving glance every time.

When it was cool and iced, she cut half the cake into man-sized chunks for Cal to take to work. He enjoyed doing that to impress his workmates, especially the bachelors for whom home cooking was a rare treat.

She smiled to herself.

Life was good again.

After making up in the customary, delightful way following their recent fight, she and Cal had grown closer for it, of that she was certain. Add in her father's promising recovery and discharge from hospital, the improvement in her mother's health, and the fact most of the jobs around the farm were up to date, and Libby had good reason to smile.

And then Cal came home with the day's mail.

'What's in the letter?' He eyed the official letterhead on the sheet of heavy white paper clutched in Libby's hand.

She flicked him a hollow-eyed glance. 'In a nutshell, the Lands Department is withdrawing approval for me to use the neighbouring common land lease for grazing purposes.'

'Is that all? From your expression I thought someone must've died.' At her frown, he said quickly, 'That's crummy grazing land anyway. Why are you so upset about losing it?'

'It's a handy holding space for stock we're waiting to truck out, so it's more about the convenience than anything else.' She scrunched up her face. 'Not only that, the free lease....'

'Yeah?'

'... was something Dad negotiated with the department years ago. And now I've gone and lost it.'

'Hang on ... do they say why they're withdrawing approval?' He extended a hand, and after a brief hesitation, she passed him the letter.

A tense silence fell as he skim-read the contents.

'This indicates you approached them about buying the land.'

She gave a tight-lipped nod.

'Then knocked back their asking price.'

'It was a ridiculous amount! I only enquired because I expected they'd be happy to offload the land for a peppercorn payment. I never dreamed they'd demand top dollar for a strip of poor, weedy, waterless ground, that's only fenced because Dad and I put the fencing in years ago. The cheek of them!'

'And let me guess ... you told them that.'

Another slow, pained nod. 'Though not in those *exact* words.'

'So....' He skimmed the rest of the text. 'It also says that since you've declined to purchase ... blah blah blah ... they're renegotiating the terms of the lease. Oh, and they're happy for you to continue as lessee at an annual cost of....' He gave a long whistle and fixed her with wide, incredulous eyes. 'Wow, that's a long way from free.'

'Yeah. And *way* more than it's worth.'

He handed back the letter. 'What'cha gonna do?'

Her expression hardened. 'The bureaucrats can keep the damn land. I'll take down the fencing—*our* fencing—and use it to section off an alternate holding space in one of my paddocks. And when the lease becomes overrun with feral blackberries and other weeds, I'll demand the department arrange for the regular clearing they insisted we do as leaseholders, but which will no longer be our responsibility.'

At his slow, dubious nod, she said crisply, 'I'll move the sold stock out tomorrow so we can start dismantling the fence.'

'Where will you move the stock to?'

'As a temporary measure, I'll section off part of the top paddock with electric fencing. That should hold them 'til the truck comes.'

'Isn't that prize-winning bull of yours in the mob?'

At the mention of Harry, Libby gave a fond smile. She had bred, nurtured, and won awards with the Hereford bull, and sold him for a record price at the recent sales much to Dave's delight. 'Yeah, but he has a healthy respect for electric fencing. And it's only for a few days. His new owners will be collecting him before the end of the week.'

'You sure about that? He is a bull, after all.'

'Harry will be fine. Now, I don't suppose you'd be able to help out tomorrow?'

'Sorry, babe.' Dropping a kiss on her head, he made for the bathroom calling over a shoulder, 'I'll be on day shift again.'

Muttering under her breath, 'Of course you will,' she trudged into the kitchen to finish making dinner.

7

Two days later Libby hurried inside to answer the jangling landline. 'Hello, Boronia Station?'

'That you, Libby?'

'Yeah. Who's this?'

'Wal, from up the road.'

One of her closer neighbours, Wally had been a regular visitor to the farm until an incident with his cattle dog. He'd brought the half-grown, undisciplined blue heeler along with him, and from the moment it discovered Sam snoozing in the garden bed, the dog wouldn't leave the cat alone.

Sam was pretty tolerant of visiting canines, but the heeler's constant prodding pushed him to the limit. With tabby fur standing on end he leapt to his feet, which spurred the dog into attack mode. With a snarl, it took off after the fleeing cat, ignoring Wally's yells to drop.

When Sam raced past her with the dog hot on his heels, Libby shouted, 'LEAVE HIM!' and lashed out with a well-aimed riding boot.

The kick to its mid-section finally got the heeler's attention. It lurched sideways with a grunt and slid to a startled stop, cringing and eyeing her with new respect. When Wally made a move toward it, the dog tucked its tail between its legs and beat a hasty retreat home.

As if he'd witnessed the performance, Sam flashed Libby what she suspected was a conspiratorial cat-grin before emerging from the corner of the house, to saunter back to his spot in the garden bed.

Although the only damage from the altercation was to canine pride, Wally wasn't impressed that Libby had kicked his dog. But when he reprimanded her, instead of receiving an apology he copped a fierce, 'What was I supposed to do, Wal? Stand by and let *your* dog savage *my* cat on *my* property?'

He'd left soon after, and hadn't been back since.

'Look,' he went on gruffly, 'I thought I'd better let you know that bull of yours is here, at my place.'

'My....' Her head jerked up. *'What?'*

'Found 'im on the road outside last night 'n brought 'im into my house yard.'

'How the hell did he get—'

'And ... well ... he's been injured.'

Her heart stopped, then gave a powerful thump and rose into her throat. *'Injured?'* she croaked. 'How? By dogs?'

'Nah, don't look like bite injuries to me. Don't think he's gone through a barbed wire fence neither. Reckon it was that gang of city kids, the ones that de-horned the Smith's longhorn steer.'

The steer, with its impressive set of horns, had become something of a tourist attraction in the area. Appearing to enjoy the attention, the quiet beast had obliged many a gawker by ambling to the fence and posing for wide-angle photos. Now it stood with mauled head drooping, appearing destined only for butchering.

'Since they've been around,' Wally continued, 'there's been a spate of attacks on stock. Seems the brainless delinquents find hurtin' animals fun. I'm bettin' it was them what had a go at your bull. And the poor bugger must've tried to fight back, 'cos he's in a pretty bad way.'

Moaning, 'Oh no ... no....' she screwed her eyes shut and put a hand to her head.

'You'd just sold 'im too, hey?'

A tight, 'Yeah,' was all she could manage.

'Sorry for bein' the bearer of bad news.'

She took a deep breath and opened her eyes. 'No need for you to apologise, Wal. And thanks for letting me know. I'll come straight down and get him.'

'Right-oh.'

'The buyers have agreed to hold off cancelling 'til we know if Harry's going to recover fully. He's still at the vet's receiving treatment for the injuries.'

'Oh hell, Lib. Those vet fees'll take a cut from your sale profits.' Dave's wincing head shake was obvious in his voice. 'What rotten timing. You just sold that bull for top dollar....' His sigh whooshed down the phone line.

'Yeah, and the truck was only a couple of days away.'

'So how did he get out of the holding paddock?'

She paused before answering. 'I'd moved the sold stock into the front paddock to wait 'til the truck came. Sectioned off an area with electric fencing,' she went on hurriedly, 'but should've put it further back from the road. I think the yobbos broke the line, not Harry. With a bit of luck, they copped a good shock from it,' she added resentfully.

'You moved the stock out of the lease?'

'Yeah. It's lucky the others stayed where they were and didn't follow him out—'

'Hang on, Lib. Why would you move the stock? We've always penned our sellers in the lease and loaded them from there.'

Bending her head she gave a slow blink and said hesitantly, 'I had to move them because ... the lease is no longer ours ... I mean mine ... to use.'

'*What*? Not ours to use anymore?' When his outburst was met with a tense silence, Dave released a breath and said more calmly, 'Sorry for shouting. Just ... tell me what happened.'

Arriving home from work that afternoon, Cal found Libby seated head in hands at the kitchen table. At his cautious, 'Lib?' she raised watery eyes to meet his.

'Dad blames me.'

'For Harry? But—'

'And for losing the lease.'

'Oh.'

'Yeah.'

Moving closer, he wrapped her in his arms. When she sagged against him, he murmured into her hair, 'Don't worry about Dave. He'll get over it.'

'It's not just that.' With a sniff, she drew back and dragged a hand over her eyes. 'Dad's still recovering from that heart scare. The last thing he needs is more stress. And while Wally Morris was a big help with the Harry thing, he also has a big mouth. By now the whole town will've heard about the incident, and about my loss of the lease. Not only am I gonna have to face the pitying glances when I'm in town, but Dad will no doubt cop more snide "Told you so" comments from his farmer mates. You might cop some ribbing too, at work. And it's all thanks to my stupidity.'

'You weren't to know some idiots were gonna have a go at your bull.'

'But I put him at risk, firstly by losing the lease, and secondly by setting up an alternative holding area too close to the road. Harry's earned himself a reputation around town after selling for a record price. I should've known better than to put him in full view of anyone going past on the road.'

'Did you report the incident to the Police?'

She nodded. 'Not sure they can do much, though.'

'Still, it's worth a try. The buggers might *kill* a beast next time.' At her distraught expression, Cal pulled her close again. 'It'll blow over, babe. Things'll be back to normal before you know it.' Resting his trendy stubbled chin on her head, he gazed unseeingly through the sliding glass doors at the farming vista outside, and a crease formed between his thick brows.

Here's hoping my *little problem blows over too.*

When Libby moved in his arms, he gave her back a distracted pat.

Then again, it could blow up in my face if that fool Don doesn't keep his yap shut.

All three knew to lie low until the trouble passed, but something Don let slip had reached the cops' ears. And having to back peddle was clearly taking a toll on Don's already jangled nerves, judging by his behaviour at the pub the night before.

When the other patrons had started glancing their way thanks to Don's raised voice, Cal hastened to frogmarch him outside and warn him yet again to keep his head down and his mouth shut. And Don had grown calmer, but Cal left the pub sure that if the pressure got too much, the bloke would cave. And if he caved he'd blab, nothing surer, and take the other two down with him.

Misery loves company.

Taking care to keep Libby's head tucked beneath his chin so she wouldn't notice his scowl, Cal raised a hand to rub the back of his neck. Paul, the third and major player in their little drama, needed to be informed of this troubling development and warned to curtail activities, but Cal hadn't been able to raise him. If he was out and about, carrying on 'business' as usual, the three entrepreneurs could wind up in a whole heap of trouble.

Damn you, Don. We were getting away scot-free 'til you opened your stupid gob.

'I hope you're right.' Libby snuggled closer. 'I don't think I can cope with any more complications right now.'

At her words he stiffened and drew back, grim-faced.

You think you've got complications? It's not like your farming dramas could see you ending up in prison. And unlike you, I don't have loved ones to dump my troubles onto.

Muttering, 'I'll get cleaned up,' he let her go and marched to the bathroom.

I have enough to worry about without being burdened by other people's crises. And let's face it, this isn't my farm, so these aren't my crises.

Standing in the shower recess, he let the water run over his coal-grimed head and body before turning to gaze moodily through the small, head-height window. As he took in the late afternoon's orange-gold glow on the horizon, the lyrics of a song by the Wolfe Brothers popped into his head.

Is it a highway sky tonight?

He frowned away the impulse but the inkling remained, dug-in like the seed of an invasive weed.

Have I stayed too long in one place?

On the back veranda, Libby too was staring fretfully at the sky. In the quiet of evening a lone magpie warbled a drowsy song. Wishing she could sing away her troubles like that, she forced a breath through tightly pursed lips. She couldn't even vent to her parents, her father being one of the issues she had to deal with ... through no fault of his own, of course.

I can't blame him for being angry and disappointed with me. I'm angry and disappointed with myself.

Hearing Cal turn off the shower, she loosened her hands from behind her head.

Even if he can't fix the problems, at least I have Cal to share them with. I should be thankful I'm not dealing with all this on my own.

She frowned.

And I wasn't totally alone before, with MJ as my fall-back and sounding board. But that clearly gave people the wrong impression, so it's fortunate—and kinder to MJ, who no doubt has troubles of his own and doesn't need mine added to the pile

—I have Cal to rely on now.

With that thought bringing her a measure of comfort, she turned and went inside.

~

'I'm sorry, mate. It just … came out—' Don gasped as Cal grabbed him roughly and hauled him out of the crib room.

Once behind the building, he shoved Don against the wall and stood stiff-legged in front of him, hands on hips, glaring. 'Did I hear you right? Did you really say my name "just came out" when you were talking to the cops?' Cal's top lip curled and he snaked out a hand to grab Don by the throat. 'You imbecile! I *knew* you'd drop us in it the instant you started to feel the heat.'

When Don managed to choke, 'I didn't … s-say you *did* anything, just that … you're a m-mate, 'n we w-work together,' Cal released his grip and curled his hand into a fist in the other man's face.

'You've gone and wrecked *everything.*' His icy blue eyes bored into Don's frightened brown ones. 'All you had to do was stick to the story the three of us agreed on. But no, you had to go blabbing like a halfwit.' His eyes narrowed further. 'Though you somehow managed to avoid mentioning Paul's name. Guess you're smart enough to know he'd kill you for implicating him.' Grabbing Don by the collar, Cal hauled his head closer and growled, 'So tell me, blabber mouth, what makes you think *I* won't do the same?'

Don cringed, and staring at Cal's raised fist blubbed, 'You wouldn't hit a mate, would ya?'

Cal's expression darkened and he spat, 'You're no mate of mine, not any more. And you deserve worse than a flogging.'

As he struggled against Cal's vice-like hold, Don's trembling mouth turned down at the edges and he snivelled, 'Go on then, give it your best shot.'

Bad move.

Cal didn't blame the first-aider who dobbed them in for fighting on the job, not really. The man was obliged to report the incident, having found himself treating a bleeding, semi-conscious Don where he lay in the dirt. No, it was Cal's own fault he'd been caught. He should've left the scene before anyone came, but Don's pathetic screams had brought people running faster than expected.

And Cal hadn't thought to wipe the blood off his fists....

8

'I don't understand.' Libby dropped the half-peeled sweet potato on the mound of peelings and whirled around to gape at him. 'You suddenly decide to quit your job and head up north to the back of Bourke, just like that? Without talking to me first?'

Cal eyed her. Should he own up to being suspended for fighting at work? But that could lead to admitting his part in starting the fire, the one that damaged a portion of her property and almost bankrupted a nearby farmer. An image flashed across his mind, of flames streaking through dry leaf litter and licking at tree trunks. He suppressed a guilty wince, recalling the sensation of the blaze's rising heat against his skin.

No, best he keep the details to himself.

'It's a terrific opportunity, Lib. Seedy Creek is an iron

ore venture, and I'll be glad to leave filthy coal mining behind. I'll also be on almost twice what I'm earning now. Think of the boost all that extra money will give us. You'll even be able to replace the ute—'

'But you'll be away most of the year.'

'I'll have regular holidays to spend here with you.'

When he stepped in to gently grasp both her arms, she scowled into his smiling, cajoling, face. 'So I'm supposed to be happy with only having you here for a whole four weeks a year?'

'Six weeks. As a shift worker I have increased leave entitlements. And it won't be forever. Just long enough to build up the farm's coffers.'

'Since when have you cared about the farm's financial situation?'

'That's a bit harsh.' He let go of her and stepped back. 'Of course I care, because *you* care. I know how much the farm means to you, Lib. Why do you think I'm doing this if not to benefit you and me, to set us up for the future?'

'Really?' She crossed her arms. 'And what do you see in our future, Cal? Aside from long, lonely stretches of being apart from each other?' Despite her determination not to let her father's opinions sway her, his words replayed in her head.

I have my doubts about a bloke who's real keen to move in with a girl but not so keen to propose to her.

Her mouth tightened in a grim line as she wrestled the thought away.

'I can tell you're upset, babe. You just need time to think this through—'

'And I can tell your mind's already made up, so my having time to think won't change anything, will it?'

He said nothing, merely blew a long-suffering breath, turned, and left the room.

Libby stood, lips quivering, staring hollowly after him.

'So the bull's gone?'

'On Wednesday. The new owners sent a truck to collect him after they received the vet's final report.'

'Harry's injuries responded well to treatment?'

'Yes, thankfully. His condition improved quickly.'

'Well that's something, I guess.'

Was it her imagination, or was there still a condemnatory edge to her father's words?

Harry's incident was weeks ago. Surely Dad's put it behind him by now, along with the kerfuffle about the lease?

Libby shook her head.

It could be the lousy phone connection making him sound officious, or just me being overly sensitive. Haven't really been myself lately....

Her nerves felt taut these days, stretched like rubber bands, only tightening further when she counted the weeks before Cal's first trip home.

He feels so far away. And not just in physical distance....

∼

Cal rolled over, groaned, and put a hand to his thumping head. He'd drunk way too much the previous evening. That was dumb, considering it was a work night. But the other blokes had insisted he not 'pike out' of his next shout of drinks ... and the next ... and the one after that. In the end, he'd forgotten all about returning to his quarters to catch some sleep, instead staying on ... and on ... in the mining camp's privately run wet mess.

I hate to think what shouting all those drinks cost me.

He groaned again.

Did my turn to buy come around more often than theirs?

Still, it felt great to be welcomed on site so enthusiastically, even if some of his new workmates were a bit ... dodgy. Like 'Snake', with the split tongue and weird, contact-lensed lizard eyes, who always stank of weed except, suspiciously, on the drug and alcohol testing days. The weirdo obviously had inside information.

Cal shuddered.

What would Libby have to say about my new mates?

A more sobering thought followed.

And about that barmaid who's always making eyes at me?

As a vague memory surfaced, he patted the pocket of his crumpled shirt and something crackled in it. After digging out a piece of paper, he stared at the name and phone number scribbled on it.

Prue.

With the name came more clarity of memory.

She'd whispered something while tucking the note in his pocket and serving him another beer. But all he could clearly recall was her warm breath against his ear, the low neckline of her clingy singlet top, and the sensation of being on a sure thing.

But ... Libby.

Libby.

She insisted on calling him most nights, and when she couldn't reach him by phone, sent 'missing you' texts and emails. Why couldn't she give him some space to settle in, come to grips with the new job and quirks of camp-based life, and make some friends?

She's lonely, I get it. But I've been gone for weeks, she should be used to it by now. I've had to make adjustments too, and I'm doing okay.

The mining camp would be his home for some time, so it was a wise move to be seen as 'one of the boys' by the predominantly male workforce. Actually, it was proving easier than expected to fall in with the single men's thinking and their oft-repeated motto, 'What happens in camp stays in camp.' A motto usually accompanied by winks and wolfish grins.

Shaking his head and straightaway regretting the rash move, Cal perched gingerly on the edge of the bed, brushing aside thoughts of the woman steadfastly waiting for him down south.

The woman counting the days, weeks, and months

before his next leave.

With a hasty glance at the bedside clock, he heaved himself to his feet and waited for his head to stop spinning.

Barely enough time to get cleaned up and clocked on.

He gave a loud burp and pulled a face at the sour, yeasty taste it left in his mouth.

Can't stomach breakfast anyhow.

Promising himself he'd hit the hay earlier that night, he shuffled to the bathroom.

Squeezing her eyes closed, Libby bent her head and pinched the bridge of her nose between thumb and forefinger. If she didn't answer their message promptly, she knew her parents would only call again.

And again.

Until they reached her.

'How's Cal going, love?' her mother asked kindly. 'Heard from him this week?'

Libby took a deep breath. 'Doing okay, I think. It's ... been a few days since I last talked to him.'

More like ten days. But I daren't hound him about being hard to reach, not after last time.

The now familiar stomach flip intensified as his angry words replayed in her head.

'It's alright for you, Lib,' he'd snapped. 'As your own boss you can work whatever hours suit. Try doing a few twelve-hour shifts in a row and see how you feel afterwards. Worn out and brain-dead is how, and about as chatty as a fence post. So don't start on me just 'cos I don't answer the phone every time it rings.'

Swallowing hard, she said quickly before her mother could respond, 'The long shifts he works knock him around a bit.' She hated sounding so defensive.

'I suppose they would,' Rhonda said carefully. 'But he gets days off in between, doesn't he?'

From across the mechanic's shed the man in high-viz work wear waved an arm above his helmeted head and yelled, 'Yo, Cal!'

Pausing on his way to the crib room, Cal called back, 'What, Rod?'

'You comin' to the Bachelors and Spinsters ball on Saturday?'

'First I heard of it.'

After being chipped during his first weeks on the job about arriving late for pre-start meetings, Cal had become more circumspect about socialising on work nights.

Rod threw him a suggestive grin. 'You know Alinta's gonna be there?'

Alinta Mason, the mine site's pay mistress. The men

made intentional mistakes on their timesheets so the eye-catching, busty blonde would visit them in their work areas. After meeting Cal in person she had run admiring eyes over the 'handsome newbie', and to the dismay of his drooling workmates, blatantly singled him out for attention from that point forward.

This earned him the outspoken envy of his workmates and a site-wide reputation as a lady's man. And it was great news for Cal as it disproved his sneaking—clearly unfounded—fear he might be losing his looks and charm. It also succeeded in heightening Alinta's appeal, which he'd so far kept within the bounds of a mild flirtation. Though there was no denying her obvious allure.

'And are you comin' to Jim's bucks night too?' Rod persisted.

'When is that on?'

'The Friday before the B 'n S.'

Cal paused with lips pursed.

Camp life could be boring as hell if a bloke didn't make the most of any and all social events.

'Yeah, I'll be there ... at both.'

'Bonza. Say, I noticed barmaid Prue's been makin' eyes at you. Reckon you could talk her into strippin' for the bucks night? Jim'll go the brightest shade of red if she starts peelin' off her gear.' Rod gave a crude guffaw.

Cal frowned. 'What makes you think she'd come at that?'

'Oh she makes like a good girl for your benefit but I've

seen Prue in action before, when she's had a few. Anyway, I reckon she'd do anything for *you*.'

Cal had a feeling Rod was right. And while he saw their to-and-fro as just another—and for him, an advantageous —flirtation, Prue clearly had other ideas and was always angling for more.

I already have a clingy woman at home. There's no way I'm getting tangled up with another.

The crease in his brow deepened.

Prue needs to get the message we're just mates, but I don't want to spoil things between us with awkward explanations. That would definitely be to my disadvantage. Her special treatment at the bar has saved me quite a bit of money already.

He brooded for a long moment, and then his expression lifted.

What if I turn up at the B 'n S with the pretty Alinta on my arm? That'd get everyone talking for sure. So even if she didn't see us together, Prue would be bound to hear the gossip and assume I'm off the menu. All without me having to say anything to her. And Alinta's already been dropping hints about the ball, so I reckon she's just waiting for me to ask her.

His eyes narrowed, took on a predatory glint as he pictured the pay mistress pressed against his side, no doubt dressed—almost—in an outfit even more revealing than her usual work wear. A lustful thrill ignited within him, followed by a surge of guilt.

But this thing with Alinta wouldn't be a real 'date', he told himself, simply a matter of convenience. If she knew another woman—meaning Prue of course—was making advances, surely Libby would applaud him for side-stepping those advances?

But she doesn't know ... and won't hear about it from me.

No point worrying her for nothing.

9

Libby took the freshly printed pages from the tray and scanned their contents.

'You still there, love?' her mother's words emanated from the phone receiver.

She returned it to her ear. 'Yes, sorry Mum. I was just grabbing a page off the printer.'

'Something important?'

'Only a copy of Cal's work roster.'

It had taken a few requests but he'd finally emailed it to her.

She continued scanning the pages, murmuring distractedly, 'He's on a two days on, three days off shift rotation.'

The first of those three days off he would no doubt spend catching up on sleep. But that left two whole days when he'd be back to something approaching normal. So why did it almost always fall on her to contact him? How long since *he'd* phoned *her* on one of his days off, simply for a chat? And why did it sometimes take him a whole week to respond to her texts or emails?

Oh, whenever they did speak he was his usual charming—if a tad preoccupied—self. And he could be forgiven for being preoccupied, having so much on his plate right now.

Am I turning into one of those insecure, demanding women who never give their men a moment's peace?

'I don't mean to pry, love,' Rhonda said gently, 'but ... we worry about you, spending so much time alone now.'

'It's no big deal. I've been on my own before this.'

'You always had MJ to call on back then.' A tense silence greeted her. 'You haven't mentioned him much lately,' Rhonda went on, choosing her words with care. 'I wondered if you and MJ might've ... well ... I thought he might've ... backed off after Cal moved in.'

'I'm not aware that he did,' Libby said stiffly, 'and if he *has* "backed off" it was by his own choice.'

'You and he have been friends all your lives, love, and he's been such a help to you in so many ways on so many occasions. You can't ... snub him simply because you have Cal now.'

'Are you implying I've kicked MJ to the long grass *again*, because someone better came along?'

'I just—'

'You don't think MJ's right to keep his distance from another man's wife—' Libby coughed. 'And *de facto* wife still counts.'

'It's not that—'

'Tell me something, Mum. How do you think Dad would feel if some other man was always calling in to help you out around the house?'

'Well ... yes, I take your point. But your father's handy. Cal's ... well, you know ... Cal.'

'And I love him for who he is, not just what he can do for me.'

'Of course you do, and that's how it should be. All I'm saying is don't burn your bridges with MJ. Good neighbours are like precious gems, you don't want to lose them.'

'Noted. And much as I'd be pleased to go on discussing the merits of male usefulness, I have work to do.' As soon as the sharp words were out Libby hung her head, wishing she could take them back.

After an injured pause Rhonda said, 'Of course, love. I'll let you get on.'

'Oh, Mum, I didn't mean to snap at you,' Libby murmured wretchedly. 'I'm sorry.'

Rhonda sighed. 'I only want you to know we care and are always thinking of you.'

'And I love you for it. Both of you.'

'We love you too, Lib.'

As she put down the phone, Rhonda heard her

husband growl from behind his newspaper, 'She's making excuses for him.'

'She loves Cal, Dave,' Rhonda said resignedly. 'So of course she'll stand up for him.'

'The inconsiderate bugger doesn't deserve her.' He gave a frustrated huff. 'She wouldn't *have* to make excuses if she'd chosen—'

'Don't.' Rhonda fixed him with a steely gaze. 'Just don't.'

'But MJ wouldn't have—'

'I know, but she didn't choose him, she chose Cal. We have to respect her decisions, even if we don't agree with them. And now I think it best we drop the subject.' When the only response was an unrepentant grunt, she urged, 'Are we agreed on that, Dave?'

After releasing an audible breath, he muttered sourly, 'Agreed.'

It felt like years, not months, since Cal's last visit to the farm, but he was finally coming home for another stretch of leave.

Libby scowled. When had she begun thinking of his returns home as visits? Just because everyone else did, that was no reason for her to join their condemnatory ranks.

Sweeping aside the troubling thoughts she went to the door and out onto the veranda, where the peppery fragrance and eye-squintingly red blossoms of the pelargonium in the front garden bed brought the usual sense of peace. That wasn't always the case, though. She recalled her mother, after planting the red pelargonium, brushing away tears on coming back indoors. And it *had* proven to be the last of her plantings before the move to the coast.

What a wrench that move had been for them both, leaving the farm and what had been their dream home.

As newlyweds, David and Rhonda Barnes had agonised over house plans for months, before finally deciding to build a south-facing, ranch-styled home positioned a short drive in from the road. By no means grand, the house was comfortable and practical, protected from the blazing summer sun and the storms and driving rains of winter by deep verandas on all four sides.

It had been their home for decades, where they'd lived, worked, and raised their daughter. A home they would've shared with their much-anticipated son too, had Ian not fallen victim to cot death at four months of age.

Libby released a wistful breath.

I SO wanted a brother when I was little. Someone to play with, follow around, learn from, pester. Someone good at fisticuffs to fight my schoolyard battles. Like the time Willie Lightning came at me, ready to flick his spit-laden spoon in my face. I was as surprised as Willie to see MJ step in and deliver a blow that had Willie bending over, gasping, the disgusting 'gag' forgotten.

A fond smile danced on her lips.

I was lucky to have MJ. He kept the bullies at bay, like a stand-in brother.

The smile slipped from her mouth.

All the more reason I feel sick when anyone suggests he and I....

Her head flew up at the sound of an approaching vehicle. Peering westward, she glimpsed a dust cloud heralding the vehicle's advance along the dirt road.

Not a small rig like Cal's ute, judging by the amount of dust it's sending up. A truck maybe? Heading for Wal's place, or Standring's appaloosa stud further on?

So where's Cal? He should be here by now.

If he's still coming....

Recalling one of his planned trips home that hadn't eventuated, and how it had taken him 'til the next day to inform her he wasn't coming after all, her face fell.

About to trudge back inside, she stiffened at the blaring of a horn.

Cal toots his horn like that.

With hope surging, she moved to the edge of the veranda, straining to see the vehicle. When the familiar ute came into view, she first beamed at the sight and then gave a perplexed frown.

Why is he towing a horse float?

Her veins turned to ice at a sudden thought.

To collect the rest of his gear? Is he moving out for good?

Her heart gave a jolting thud.

Hang on. He didn't leave much here, certainly not enough to warrant hiring a float.

She put a hand to her racing heart.

Calm down.

Closing her eyes, she brought to mind the grounding technique Rhonda had taught her, to help relieve anxiety attacks in the lead-up to final year exams at school.

Use your senses to ground you in the now.

She inhaled deeply of the blossom-filled air, opened her eyes to gaze at the sky, wriggled her toes in her boots, and listened to the soothing warbling of a nearby magpie.

Anyway, why would Cal be happy tooting if he's only here to quit the farm for good? He knows how devastating news like that would be to me.

Devastating?

Utterly.

When a grinning Cal climbed down from the ute Libby rushed into his open arms, almost knocking him off his feet.

'Easy, babe!' he said fondly. 'Give a man a minute to get his land legs again. Been stuck in the driver's seat staring at white lines for a whole lot of hours y'know.'

'Sorry, Cal.' She flashed a chagrined smile. 'I just ... wasn't sure it was you coming along the road. But it was, and here you are! Oh, I'm SO glad to have you home.' While staying within the circle of his arms, she drew back to gaze into his face. He didn't meet her eyes, and there was something in his expression she couldn't quite read. The closest guess was....

Guilt?

What would he have to be guilty about?

Being a lousy communicator, no doubt.

She gave a wry grin and ran assessing eyes over the rest of him. Had he put on weight, maybe even developed a hint of beer belly? She returned her gaze to his face. Had the lines around his eyes and mouth—lines she knew he detested—deepened while he was away? He hadn't been gone all that long, so she must simply be seeing them with fresh eyes. Still, wasn't he a bit young to be developing wrinkles? He only had a few years on her.... Realising she was staring when he fingered the lines on his forehead, she said quickly, 'It's just *so* wonderful to have you home again.'

'And not just me.' He dropped his hand and stepped back, waggling eyebrows at her. 'I brought someone with me. A surprise.'

Doubt clouded the shine in her eyes. 'You brought someone ... here?' Her voice crackled with tension. 'Who?'

Moving to the rear of the float, he said, 'Come see.'

She followed, frowning. 'Whose float is this?'

'Borrowed it from a bloke at work.'

'Oh.' Swallowing, she said tightly, 'So ... it's some*thing* you brought home, not some*one*?'

10

'Surprise!' As he dropped the ramp, the galloway inside the float gave a startled snort and threw up its head. Libby stared wide-eyed at the horse's twitching palomino hide and then at Cal, who beamed expectantly at her.

'Well, what do you think of your new steed?' He waved a hand at the float's occupant.

'You're ... giving me a horse?'

'Yeah, a real beauty isn't she.' It was a statement rather than a question.

'Well ... I....'

When nothing more was forthcoming he shook his head at her and, still grinning, jogged up the ramp to unfasten the halter rope. The horse gave another nervous snort at his proximity, the whites of its eyes showing.

Calling, 'C'mon, check her out,' he untied the knot and

prepared to unload the palomino, which gave a toss of its head and proceeded to rush down the ramp, dragging him with it.

Libby watched the horse dance at the end of the rope and half-rear when Cal checked it. 'Is she broken?'

'Of course,' he puffed, feet slipping in the gravel as he shortened the lead rope and attempted to calm the white-eyed animal.

Murmuring, 'Only just,' Libby moved closer to examine the horse, noting the broad, slightly dished head and, despite her nervousness, the kind look about the mare's dark eyes.

'Pretty, hey?' Cal said gleefully. 'She's an Australian stock horse. Name's Sans Rouge.'

'Mmm.'

'Thought she'd be great for your endurance riding.' At Libby's noncommittal nod his grin vanished. 'You're not saying much.' He frowned. 'Don't you like her?'

'Of course I do.' She flashed an apologetic smile and stepped in to hug him. 'Thank you, Cal, for this lovely gift.' Her words sounded tight even to her own ears. She coughed to clear her throat of the ridiculous lump that had lodged itself there.

Ridiculous, because it was always the same at even the slightest hint of a gift from Cal. Hope would raise its *pathetic* head in heart-thumping anticipation that he'd drop to one knee and open a small velvet box, to reveal the breathtaking glint of sunlight off gems....

Why did the thought even occur to her? Was a ring really so important, or was she simply desperate to prove to her parents and other doubters, in the most obvious way, that Cal was dinkum about their future together?

She swallowed and firmed her wavering smile. 'I just ... wasn't expecting you to buy me a ... horse.'

At his disconcerted frown, heat rose in her throat and face. Had her expression given away her thoughts? Her ridiculous, pitiable, hopeful thoughts?

'About that.' Bending his head, he scuffed the toe of a boot in the dirt. 'I didn't exactly *buy* the horse.'

So that's why he looked disconcerted. 'Whew!

'Oh?' With an absurdly unsteady hand she swept a lock of hair off her forehead. 'So how *did* you come by her?'

'One of the blokes at the mine got a job on an oil rig, and needed to find a home for his horses before leaving town. Tried to sell 'em but most people up there don't wanna be saddled with animals.' He gave a bark of laughter. '*Saddled,* get it?' Having received the expected—if not overly enthusiastic—response of wry amusement, he went on. 'Anyway, when he offered to give 'em away, I thought of you. Got in early to pick the best of 'em.' He handed her the lead rope.

'Right. Well .... thanks again.' Libby ran a tentative hand down the mare's pale gold face. 'She's certainly a looker.'

'Why don't you take her for a spin?'

'Later. I'll let her get settled in the yard first. And I'm

sure you're hanging out for a cuppa after travelling all this way.'

'You know it! But make it a beer, hey?' Going to the ute, he grabbed his duffel off the back seat. 'Need to wash the dust outta my throat with something cold.'

As he strode toward the house, she led the mare to the round yard, murmuring, 'C'mon, girl. Let's get you set up with water and a hay net.'

Once they were in the yard, she removed the halter and the horse flung itself away from her to career around the perimeter, silver mane flying and tail raised like a flag.

Shaking her head and muttering, 'Barely broken at best,' Libby hung up the halter and rope, before slipping through the rails and making for the house.

The following morning Cal found Libby standing outside the yard, one foot on the bottom rail and chin resting on her folded arms, gazing at her new horse. The mare had her nose buried in the feed bin, one hoof pawing the ground as she ate.

When Cal came to stand beside Libby the horse raised her head to snort bits of lucerne chaff into the air. 'See?' he said proudly. 'She's calm and settled in her new home.'

Libby didn't shift her gaze from the mare's twitching skin. 'More settled than yesterday, but I wouldn't say she's calm.'

'Oh come on.' Cal nudged her. 'Gonna take her for a ride?'

'I don't know. It might still be a bit soon.'

'But I wanna see how Sans Rouge goes for you, and I'm only here for a few days.'

'Rouge. I'm just calling her Rouge.' She eyed him levelly. 'And I'm not prepared to get on her until I'm sure she's calm. Can't afford to be thrown and injured.'

He gave an impatient huff. 'What if I get on her first?'

'You can't afford to be out of action either.'

'I'm not gonna get thrown.' He also wasn't going to let the matter drop, after all the trouble he'd gone to sourcing a gift he hoped would ease his conscience....

Thrusting away the mental images of his drunken, uninhibited behaviour at the B and S ball up north, and the equally boozy 'recovery breakfast' the day after, he said gruffly, 'I told you she's been broken,' and climbed through the timber rails. 'Come on, scaredy cat. Grab your gear and let's get her saddled.'

Rouge took a bit of catching but stood quietly enough while they got her ready to ride. She made no protest when Cal put his weight in the stirrup and swung into the saddle, further chipping away at Libby's doubts. But when he put his heels against her sides, the mare snorted and shot forward.

'Take it easy, Cal,' Libby warned as he collected the excitable mount and crab-jogged out of the yard. 'And she's not shod, so stick to the sand tracks.'

When he called, 'Right-oh,' over a shoulder, Rouge tossed her head and broke into a sprightly trot.

Libby watched until they disappeared up the road before checking and closing the tack shed.

Rouge is a good-looking horse, no question. Even if Cal got her as a freebie, it was nice of him to think of me. I should be more grateful for the gift.

She was backing the tractor out of the machinery shed a short while later when movement on the road caught her eye. Braking, she peered closer.

Cal?

Cal, trudging toward the front gate, his hatless head bent.

Back already? And why was he on foot?

She frowned, switched off the ignition, and jumped down from the Fergie. Striding to meet him she called, 'What happened? Where's Rouge?'

With an angry snort he lifted his head and shook it. 'Damn nag shied at nothin'. Threw me and then bolted.'

So now the 'real beauty' is a nag.

Libby swallowed a grin. 'You okay?'

'I'll live, though I copped one to the face when the damn thing threw its head.'

And an 'it' instead of a 'she'.

'And I have no idea where it got to.' He rubbed his forehead gingerly. 'Took off before I could catch it.'

Libby leaned in. 'Yeah, it looks like your nose is already swelling. Possibly your top lip as well. Better come inside.'

He followed her, swearing under his breath and brushing dust off his backside with both hands. 'I'll get you another gift, Lib,' he ground out. 'One that won't run off.'

Her heart melted at the swollen-lip lisp creeping into his words. 'Any idea where she ran off to?'

'Was leggin' it up the road, toward your neighbour's farm.'

MJ's place.

'Let's not worry about Rouge for the moment. Right now we need to get some ice on that face.'

Cal was stretched out on the lounge, towel-wrapped ice pack on his chiselled but now swelling and decidedly dour face, when Libby heard the jingle of a jointed bit and the clop of hoof beats outside.

Going to the door, she saw a rider astride a palomino approaching at a gentle lope along the access road. The man's tall, lean form sat easy in the stock saddle, and he rode with a loose rein, mount relaxed under his calm control.

'Is that Rouge?'

At her exclamation, Cal lifted the pack off his face and raised his head to frown at her. 'What?'

'I think MJ's here, on Rouge.'

'So she *did* go there. Well, bully for MJ,' Cal said sourly, slumping back to re-position the ice pack. 'If the nag likes his place so much, maybe he should keep the damn thing.'

With a quelling frown in Cal's direction, Libby went out to meet MJ.

'See you found my runaway mare.'

'So she *is* yours. Thought I recognised the tack.' He brought the horse to a stop and slipped down from the saddle.

Rouge stood at his side quietly blowing, sweat drying in crusted white lines on her pale gold coat.

Flipping the reins over the mare's lowered head, MJ said, 'Came belting in through the gate and up to my mob in the yard.' As he spoke he ran a hand down the horse's neck. 'Figured from the empty saddle someone had taken a tumble.' He flicked a glance over Libby's clean face and clothes. 'I take it that wasn't you?'

She shook her head. 'Cal was riding her.'

'He okay?'

'Copped a blow to the face.' She gave a conspiratorial grin and lowered her voice. 'And to his pride. But he'll be alright.'

MJ handed her the reins. 'Right then. I'd best be gettin' back. Got a load of hay arrivin' this morning.'

'Can I give you a ride home?'

His lips twitched. 'On the Fergie?'

'No.' Sweeping an errant strand of sun-bronzed brunette hair off her brow, she arched an eyebrow at him. 'I'd treat you to a trip in the ute.'

'Thanks for the offer, but I'll take the shortcut across

the paddocks.' His mouth firmed and something akin to doubt settled on his face. 'If ... that's okay by you?'

Was this the same MJ who, like her, had crossed the boundary so often it no longer felt like a dividing line between their properties? The MJ who knew the number of fence posts between his place and hers, having counted them years ago?

'What kind of question is that? Since when do you need permission to cross my land?'

'Since you ... and ... er....'

His voice trailed off but she got his meaning, and heard her mother's voice in her head.

Seems you were right again, Mum. He has backed off.

'It's always been fine for you to cut across my paddocks whenever you like, MJ, and always will be. So don't ask again. We clear on that?'

He dipped his dark head. 'Clear.'

'Now I'd better see to this horse. Oh, and thanks so much for bringing her back.'

'No trouble. By the way, she seems a bit green. Let me know if you want her schooled some more.'

'Will do, thanks. She's such a pretty thing, I *would* like her quieted enough to show.'

Though I might leave it 'til after Cal's gone back up north. Something tells me he wouldn't be too keen on having MJ school his 'gift' horse.

As she led the mare to the yard, Libby watched MJ

stride across the paddock, his long, blue-jeaned legs eating up the distance between their two homesteads.

He has such a quiet way about him, horses quickly learn to trust him.

And not just horses....

11

Outside, water splashed from the overflowing gutters to plop into deepening puddles in every indentation in the sandy ground. Libby stood with the phone pressed to her ear, gazing out at the rain sheeting from the leaden sky. The farmer in her was glad of the tank-replenishing, paddock-greening downpour, while the woman in her stared dully into the grey wetness, her mind far away.

Then her call was answered and her eyes lit up. She opened her mouth to speak, only to have a recording announce jauntily in her ear, 'Gidday, cobber. You've reached Cal's phone. You know the drill. Leave a message after the beep and I'll get back to you when I can.'

Her face fell. While loving the sound of his voice, she had come to loathe that *damned* message. 'Cal, it's me,' she said after the beep. Hearing the sharpness in her tone, she made an effort to soften it. 'Are you getting my messages? I've left a couple now.' The crease in her brow deepened and she bent her head to stare at the floor. 'Anyhow ... call me when you get a chance. Missing you.' She hung up but kept hold of the receiver, tapping it against her chin.

Cal had been back at work for a month and a half, and despite promising to stay in more regular contact before he left, was once more proving hard to reach. It seemed some of his promises came with use-by dates.

He'd even said he'd write to her, but the one letter she received was a brief, one page missive, that said things were 'okay' up there, that he was 'doing okay', that work was 'okay'. Where were the reassurances she craved, the 'Miss you, can't wait to get home again', and the 'PS - I love you', in flourishes of his elaborate handwriting?

With a shake of her head, she thumped the receiver back into its cradle.

There I go again, thinking badly of him, even after he gifted me a beautiful horse. And I didn't even ride Rouge while he was here, which obviously disappointed him. Though maybe not as much after he was thrown and left in the dirt.

Her mouth tipped into a lopsided grin, and then she sobered.

I shouldn't laugh, his swollen nose and lip were sore for ages. Anyway, I'll make it up to him once Rouge has had some proper schooling. Then I'll be glad to show her off to him.

Lifting her gaze, she stared out through the falling rain to the low eastern escarpment, the Darling Scarp. Shrouded in darkening storm clouds, its hills were barely visible.

Was this to be her lot in life, weathering every storm alone?

Frowning, she sucked in her bottom lip.

Why did she have to fall for a bloke who then decides to spend most of the year away working?

And Cal wasn't just away. He was very, *very* far away, where there was no telling what was going on, especially when he rarely answered his phone. And it wasn't as if he'd go unnoticed by any single women on site.

He had both looks and charm in spades.

The alarm blared its unwelcome message.

Sucking in a peeved breath, Cal blinked his eyes open and groaned. He'd been back on site six weeks and should be well into the swing of his shift roster again, but the earlies were always the hardest. He dragged a hand over his face and glanced at the clock, already knowing what it would tell him but hoping for a reprieve of some sort. Maybe the clock was fast?

It wasn't.

With another groan he rose and headed to the bathroom. As he stood under the shower, letting the steaming water cascade over his head and body, images from the dream flooded back to fill his mind.

There was no mistaking the blonde woman in the starring role.

No mistaking her at all....

Grasping the hot water tap with a dripping hand he turned it fully off, to stand shivering as the water lost its warmth. The chill had the desired effect, and along with the heat-dousing influence came clarity of thought.

It was only a dream. The guilt he was feeling—about something he hadn't actually done, had only dreamed about doing—was absurd, irrational, and not worth a second thought.

I bet Libby has dreams about other men. And I know Alinta dreams about me, she told me so herself. All I'm doing is returning the favour.

The pricking of his conscience weakened into a feeble nudging.

Why suffer an attack of the guilts when I've done nothing wrong?

The nudging receded further until barely discernible.

And who can blame a bloke for dreaming about gorgeous women?

Alinta's coquettishly pouting face flashed into his mind.

Sure beats the nightmares I had after that close call down south when Don, the loose-lipped idiot, almost brought trouble sniffing at my door.

Cal gave a loud sniff himself.

He should be glad he only got a beating. Would've copped far worse if he'd implicated Paul.

With a self-satisfied grunt, Cal turned the hot water tap back on.

'Got a stretch of fencing wire needs replacing on the sou'east corner.' Libby stood with the phone to her ear a few days later, only this time her call had been answered by a person. 'Any chance you could give me a hand some time, when the weather fines up?'

'Sure, and it looks like the rain's gone for the time being.' MJ's words rumbled over the line.

Even as a young boy he'd had a manly voice, another thing about him she'd always admired.

'I've got some free time this arvo?'

She smiled at his ready response. 'That'd be super ... if you're sure I'm not imposing?'

'Remember chewing me out the other day for asking a dumb question?'

She gave a wry huff. 'Yeah, right-oh. See you this afternoon. Come to the house first, hey?'

'Shall do.'

When he arrived, she was surprised to see him riding Rouge. The mare moved with ease, supple rather than edgy under saddle, and stood calmly mouthing the bit while he dismounted.

After tucking the bulging fencing gloves firmly into the back pocket of his paint-spattered cargo pants, he lifted the turned-down brim of his Akubra hat with one finger and nodded a greeting at Libby. When he walked toward her, steel-capped work boots on his feet instead of the usual riding boots, the mare followed without being prompted.

'Gidday, MJ.'

'Lib.'

She watched him push the long sleeves of his khaki shirt into wads at his tanned elbows, and then moved her gaze to the horse. 'Rouge is looking way more relaxed.'

'Yep. Shaping up well after somethin' of a shaky start. Had to take her back to basics. Don't think whoever gentled her really knew what they were doin'.'

'You done working her?'

'Not quite. Wanna take her through the bush on unfamiliar tracks 'n see how she handles that.'

Libby nodded.

'Say, how about you come along? Shorty would be a calming influence.' MJ glanced at the gelding standing dozing in the house paddock. 'And judgin' by that round belly, he could use the exercise. His leg's fully healed, isn't it?'

'Yeah, been good for a while now.'

'So, what d'ya say?'

'It's tempting ... feels like ages since I went for a pleasure ride.' She paused to tap fingers against her lips. 'Where are you planning to go?'

'Doc's place.'

A well-known local, Doc Studsor carried on his equally well-known family's tradition of breeding and training pacers.

'Got a tool I need to return,' MJ went on, 'one he lent me a while ago. Don't want him thinkin' I'm one of those "lending equals keeping" buggers.'

'I'm sure he wouldn't think that. No one who knows you would.'

MJ gave a grunt. 'His place is a half-day's ride there and back through the bush, on sand tracks all the way. You up for it?'

'When?'

'Next Saturday afternoon?'

Libby stared into his familiar, unshaven face, searching for ... an ulterior motive?

What's wrong with me?

MJ wasn't just any bloke, he was a long-time friend and neighbour. Someone she trusted more than almost anyone else, who she'd been with on maybe hundreds of rides over the years. So why was she hesitating now? Could it be she was letting what others thought about their long-time friendship sow seeds of doubt in her own mind?

She resisted the impulse to scowl.

What kind of idiot would that make me?

Lifting her chin, she flashed him a smile. 'Next Saturday should be fine.'

'Great. Be ready for a chat. I'm sure Doc'll have the kettle on.'

The smile fell from her lips. 'Did he hear about Shorty's floating injury?'

Doc had gifted her the ex-pacer, racing name Mister Shortstuff, after the gelding's inauspicious and correspondingly brief racing career ended. Having bred and trained him, Doc still took a keen interest in Shorty, and viewed his accomplishments with pride. Would he think her negligent for not bandaging the horse for floating?

'Well *I* haven't mentioned it.'

She gave a tense nod and glanced at the mare. 'Do you want to put Rouge in the round yard? We'll take the ute to the fencing job. Got all the tools loaded in it already.'

'Right-oh.'

'And speaking of kettles, fancy a cuppa before we head out? So happens I just took a batch of honey oat bars out of the oven.' When he smacked his lips, she grinned. MJ always had been a sucker for the crunchy, fruit and honey-packed slices.

It was the first recipe her mother had suggested she make when, as a little girl, Libby wanted to try her hand at baking. And a young MJ had happily joined the ranks of guinea pigs, perching at the kitchen table beside Dave, napkin tucked into the neck of his checked shirt, and cup of sugared black tea—still his hot drink of choice—in front of him. He had eyed the sweet slices cooling on the rack with unbridled expectation, and been happily eating them ever since, whenever they were on offer.

For that matter, Libby couldn't recall him ever knocking back *any* offer of home cooking. Of course he had no 'little woman in the kitchen' to bake for him, after his mother's move to Perth some years ago.

'You beauty. A bloke needs to keep his strength up, 'specially when there's fencin' to be done.' There was gratitude and something akin to relief in his grin, making her wonder if he too had regretted the recent shift in their relationship.

'Right then. Come inside after you put Rouge away.'

'Okay, boss.'

A short while later he trooped into the sunny kitchen, having first dumped his hat and boots by the door and washed his hands under an outside tap. Padding in socked feet to the worn but solid timber table, he pulled out a chair and sat to watch Libby brew a pot of tea.

Without looking up, she said idly, 'Had a close encounter with a dugite the other day.'

MJ frowned. 'How close?'

While not as aggressive as the tiger snakes that were the district's more notorious slithery residents, the highly venomous dugites could kill with one bite.

'Almost stood on it.' She glanced at him, suppressing a fond smile at the sight of his flat, sweat-blackened, hat hair.

'Almost?'

'Yeah. We both survived the encounter.'

He released a breath in an audible whoosh. 'Where was it?'

'Right outside the feed shed, probably on the hunt for mice. Reckon it got as big a fright as I did when I bowled around the corner from the round yard.' She thrust an arm to the side, finger pointed. 'It took off one way at a great rate of knots, while I went,' and she thrust out the other arm, 'the opposite way, at an even greater rate of knots.'

'Best outcome for both of you.' MJ settled back in the chair, hands behind his head, a smile twitching the edges of his firm mouth. Opportunities for neighbourly chit-chats with Libby had dried up lately, so he was determined to savour the moment.

'Yep.' She paused, holding a spoonful of tea leaves in the air above the pot. 'Oh, and you know that young roo, the little buck with a floppy ear?'

'The one you pulled out of the hole a while ago?'

The nearby forest was dotted with areas of ground subsidence, some holes deep enough to trap a man. The locals knew to give these remnants of underground mine workings a wide berth, but wildlife occasionally fell victim to them.

The joey, possibly trying out his new legs too close to the hazard, was lucky Libby came upon the scene while out riding. After swinging down from the saddle, she moved cautiously to the edge of the hole and dropped to her stomach. With its mother watching anxiously from a safe distance, she managed to grab the exhausted youngster by the scruff and haul him to safety.

'That's him, and he's not a joey anymore.' She tipped the leaves into the pot and scooped another spoonful from the tin. 'He's getting bigger and bolder. Came right up to me the other day. I had an empty carton in my hand and bonked him on the nose with it when he got too close. Didn't hurt him at all, just sounded scary. Anyway, he got the message and took off.'

'Wise move. You don't want the males getting too "friendly". The buggers can turn nasty after they've matured. Case in point, Bobby Wilson.'

A local wildlife carer, generally considered a goodhearted bloke if not the sharpest tool in the box, Wilson had taken in a Western Grey kangaroo after it was struck by a car. Thanks to the care it received the young buck recovered well from its injuries, but Wilson hesitated when the time came to return his latest 'pet' to the wild.

That all changed the day the buck's unprovoked attack during feeding time put Wilson in hospital, and led to the animal's release being fast-tracked. Wilson never forgot the lesson learned. The permanent scarring on his face and body wouldn't let him forget it.

Nodding agreement, Libby dropped the last spoonful of tea leaves into the pot.

The familiar, grassy scent of the leaves, combined with the lingering aroma of recent baking, the whistle of the kettle, the clink of china mugs, and the companionable chitchat, brought to mind all the times MJ had spent in the kitchen's welcoming comfort.

He'd lost count of the hours spent there, talking farming with Dave and more recently Libby, over home-baked muffins or slabs of buttered fruit cake.

Until Callum McDougall came on the scene and re-wrote the script.

When a flicker of resentment crossed his face, MJ hastily focused his gaze on the hand-knitted cosy Libby was slipping over the teapot. Years of use had faded the woollen cosy, but it still sported a large fabric flower on one of its rather uneven sides. He recalled the young, piggy-tailed Libby twirling the finished cosy on a finger, and beaming with pride when first his mum and then he praised her handiwork.

Back when they were kids, and best mates.

He raised his eyes and watched her step into the walk-in pantry, to collect a dented metal cake tin from among the jars of preserved fruits, chutneys, and jams in neat rows on a shelf.

After carrying the tin to the bench, she prised open the lid and tumbled golden-brown honey oat bars onto a plate. Setting the plate in front of him with a smiling 'help yourself' lift of her chin, she collected the teapot and two brightly coloured mugs from the bench.

As she carried them to the table, a waft of air through the window ruffled the aromatic leaves of the potted mint, rosemary, and basil plants on the sun-drenched windowsill behind her. The breeze brought with it the sweet notes of a magpie's song accompanied by the lowing of nearby cattle.

Deep contentment swelled within MJ. As a boy he'd enjoyed this room's sunny, aromatic homeliness, and as a man he felt more at home here than in his own, perfectly functional kitchen ... in his whole house, to be completely honest.

Any time spent here in her kitchen, or *anywhere* in her home, was to be treasured.

As long as *she* was here too.

12

'Heard somefing interestin' the other day, I did. 'Bout that new bloke.'

The old man's words didn't register with MJ until the man's equally elderly friend asked, 'Which new bloke?' and was told, 'You know. The one who's been cartin' out the Barnes girl.'

The Barnes girl? Were they talking about Libby?

MJ froze with his hand still in the open mail box.

Though it wouldn't stay quiet for long, the post office agency was enjoying a late morning lull, so the three men had the veranda area, where the locked mail boxes lined the wall, to themselves.

The second man sniffed, took the rolled cigarette dangling from his downturned mouth, and spat tobacco flakes into the air. 'Y'mean the good-lookin' bloke what thinks 'e's better'n everyone else?'

'That's the blighter.'

When the smoker glanced his way, MJ withdrew his hand and pretended to flip through his mail.

Recognising him as a local, the man lost interest and turned his attention to the soggy cigarette hanging limply from his bony, nicotine-stained fingers. After flicking the end and managing to re-light it, he stuck the fag between his lips again and addressed his buddy. 'That bloke's livin' with 'er, ain't 'e? On the farm?'

'You sayin' he took up residence there?'

'Yeah, a while back. And Dave Barnes still ain't 'appy 'bout it neither, 'specially as the good-for-nuffing bloke ain't inclined to help around the farm. But what can a father do? Young women these days, they're gonna do what they're gonna do, 'n won't be told otherwise.' He shook his head, pushed back his sweat-stained hat with a thumb, and tongued the fag to the other side of his mouth. 'The bloke's not spendin' much time there, though. Works away a lot.'

'Yeah, up north in the mines.' The first man scratched his steel-grey beard. 'And while up there, the mongrel's makin' like a single bloke.'

MJ's hand stilled.

'You sayin' e's playin' the field?'

'That's what I heard.'

'Says who?'

'Me granddaughter's fella. 'E works up there too.'

'Reckon shenanigans like that'd go on a lot in them minin' camps.'

The first man continued rubbing his beard. 'Reckon so.'

'Cosy little setup. One girl down 'ere 'n another one up there.'

'Maybe more'n one. Y'never know with a bloke like that.'

The smoker inhaled, coughed, and squinted through the exhaled smoke. 'Can't imagine sheilas workin' on a mine site would be all that pretty, though.'

'Well accordin' to me granddaughter's fella, there's one works in the office who's a real looker.'

'Better than the bastard deserves.'

'Yep, 'n the Barnes girl don't deserve to be two-timed.'

'Y'got that right.'

'Bet she don't know 'bout what's goin' on up there neither.'

The smoker grunted agreement. 'And I wouldn't be the one to tell 'er. A man can bring a heap of trouble on 'imself by doin' that.'

'Y'got that right, Smithy. Interferin' like that always leads to trouble.'

They stood in thoughtful silence, one man stroking his beard, the other sucking on the remains of his damp rollie.

Then the first man sighed. 'Anyways, I'd best be gettin' on. Got a bit to do in town this mornin'.'

'Right-oh, Mick.'

'Be seein' ya, Smithy.'

As they shuffled off MJ stared unseeingly at the mail in his hand, telling himself that only a fool listens to small town gossip.

But was the gossip right? Was Cal doing wrong by Libby?

Where there's smoke it's a safe bet there's fire, even if only a smoulder.

The crease in his brow deepened. Suspecting the smooth-talking operator of having questionable integrity was one thing, accusing him of outright cheating was something else entirely.

And devastating news for the person being cheated on.

He pictured Libby's face after they'd finished the fencing job a few days ago. While she'd appeared heart-wrenchingly grateful for his help, he'd glimpsed something like disappointment beneath her smile. Not with the job or him—at least he hoped that wasn't the case—but perhaps at having to continue relying on others for help because her man was never around?

The unworthy bastard's a long way short of good enough for her, but it's obvious she loves him.

Scowling, MJ pressed work-hardened fingers to his temple, wishing he hadn't overheard the conversation.

If she knew what was being said she'd be devastated, no question, and completely shattered if there's truth to the talk.

He stared at the foot traffic-worn timber floor and banged the toe of a boot into an uneven plank, over and over, harder each time.

Libby deserves to know what's being said behind her back, but who'll be the one to tell her?

Recalling her reaction, back when they were teenagers, to his warning about pretty-boy Aaron's two-timing ways, he gave a grim snort.

I thought she was winding up to king-hit me, and that was back when we were able to talk about things like that. Now....

He stilled his foot, lifted his chin, and slapped the bundle of mail against his other hand.

One thing's for sure, I'd be checking the facts before I opened my mouth. And even then I'd be talking my way into a truckload of trouble and hurt feelings, nothing surer. But how can I just stand by and do nothing?

'Hello, Boronia Station.'

'I'd like to speak with Elizabeth Barnes please,' a man said crisply, his tone firm and businesslike.

A crease formed between Libby's brows. 'Speaking.'

'Sergeant Tony Wentworth here, of Brunswick Junction Police.'

She straightened and pressed the phone receiver closer to her ear. 'Yes, Sergeant?'

'You can call me Tony.'

'Okay, and I'm Libby.'

'Thanks Libby. Now, I'm phoning with regard to an

incident you reported to this office a while back, of malicious injury to livestock.'

'Yes, my bull. Do you have something to report?'

'Of a kind.' He cleared his throat. 'Our investigations have led us to some ... possible ... suspects. I say "possible" because our suspicions are as yet unsubstantiated.'

'And?'

'I felt you should be informed of the situation,' he replied stiffly. 'The individuals are still in the local area, so we're advising all residents to keep a close eye on their properties and stock.'

'I see. And you'll be taking them into custody before they strike again?'

'At this stage there's little hope we'll find sufficient evidence to pursue the teenagers in question, for that particular offence.' The frustration was obvious in the sergeant's voice.

At her deflated, 'So they're going to get away with it,' he charged on. 'Yours is not the first local incident we've earmarked them for, nor the most serious, and we're still looking into all of them.'

'Serious? Oh, you're thinking the recent fire might've been their doing too?'

'It's another line of investigation we're pursuing ... though to be honest, I doubt their involvement in such a serious case. To date they're only suspected of committing minor offences. Drunken shenanigans in town, anti-social mischief, thefts from farm sheds, that sort of thing.'

'I wouldn't class attacking my bull as a "minor" offence,' she said sharply. 'Apart from the animal's suffering, and the expensive vet bill, it could've cost me a sale worth thousands of dollars.'

'And I wasn't suggesting it was minor, by any means. Being from the country myself, I understand how you feel.' He let those words sink in before continuing. 'Like I said, we only *suspect* these individuals *could* be responsible. They may've had nothing at all to do with the attack on your beast. But assuming they *were* responsible, it'd be the worst thing they've done so far. Apart from the fire of course, and we have no proof they were involved in that either.'

'Do you think they're becoming bolder?'

'It's possible.' He sniffed. 'Unwise to make any assumptions at this point, however.'

'So your investigations are continuing?'

'Yes, though....' He paused before saying slowly, 'Unless new details come to light....'

'Let me guess. There's nothing much else you can do at this stage.'

His sigh whooshed over the phone line.

'I see. Well, can you at least tell me this, Sergeant Tony? When you say the culprits are still in the area, can you be more specific about where?'

'They have a camp at—' He stopped abruptly, but Libby had already run through possible campsite options in her head.

The most likely prospect for a no-good gang of young hoodlums? The Rayner place.

As long as they paid for the privilege, Will Rayner was known to let anyone camp on his property. His homestead was far enough away from the cleared camping area to not be bothered by the loud music, drunken screaming matches, 'cowboy ute' burn-out competitions, and other loutish camper behaviour.

The lighting of fires was the one thing Rayner was strict about, though that didn't stop some idiots from trying him on occasionally ... and being thrown out on their ears with no refund of their money.

The sergeant cleared his throat. 'Look, for now all you need to do is stay alert and contact the station if you suspect any trouble.'

She gave a snort and said dully, 'Right.'

At her aggrieved tone he went on resolutely, 'I'm only sharing our suspicions with you now because there could be a continued threat to stock and property. That said, I must reiterate that there is insufficient proof on which to base any claims of wrongdoing by *any* party.'

'Right,' she said again.

Hearing her resigned sigh, his tone softened a notch. 'I would've liked to have had better news for you.'

'You and I both. Well, thanks for the update.'

'You're welcome. Have a good day, Libby.'

'You too.' As she set the receiver back in the cradle, Libby caught the sounds of a vehicle accelerating away from the farm, and frowned when her insides gave an apprehensive flutter.

Alarmed by the sound of a car? No way!

Sticking out her chin, she strode to the door.

All this talk about perpetrators and criminal activities has put me on edge, that's all. It won't last.

She wrenched open the door and stepped out, nearly tripping as she strained to glimpse the departing vehicle amid the cloud of dust. With an irritated huff she made to go back inside, only to stop when her foot brushed against the item she'd almost tripped over.

A parcel.

Just sitting there, on the front doormat.

She stared at it, and then peered down the road again.

Was that the vehicle she'd heard, someone delivering this? But why a doorstep delivery when all her mail went to the box at the post office agency?

After a final hasty glance around, she bent to scrutinise the parcel. Wrapped in printed paper fastened by grubby pieces of sticky tape, it had her name scrawled across it in thick pencil. The same dark graphite circled a paragraph of text on the paper. Mystified, she scooped up the parcel, noting its lightness, and carried it into the kitchen. Setting it on the table, she examined all four sides.

No sender's address, post mark, or even a delivery address, just her name. Clearly the parcel had been hand-delivered from its point of origin, wherever that was.

Blowing a frustrated breath, she read the circled paragraph.

'IN ORDER TO EXPERIENCE THEIR HEALING PROPERTIES, GARNETS SHOULD BE WORN ON THE BODY. THE STONES' BENEFITS INCLUDE DETOXIFICATION OF NEGATIVE EMOTIONS, ENHANCEMENT OF THE LAWS OF ATTRACTION, AND THE DEEPENING OF EXISTING LOVE. THE GEMS ALSO SYMBOLISE CONSTANCY IN FRIENDSHIPS.'

What the hell?

Taking care not to tear the paper more than was necessary, in case the delivery had to be returned—but to where, when there was no return address?—she proceeded to unwrap the parcel. Beneath the paper she found a cardboard carton, and inside it, crumpled wads of newspaper.

Was someone playing a joke? Had she been sent a box of newspaper?

She'd seen that done to one of her friends at a party, but the pranksters had been there to laugh at the unlucky birthday girl's reaction. Who was here to witness hers?

On impulse, she swept a suspicious gaze around the room's corners and ceiling, before stopping to berate herself for being an idiot. As if someone would go so far as to plant a hidden video camera in her house! And if it *were* a prank, why pick today to deliver the parcel? It wasn't her birthday, or April Fools day, or any other special occasion.

Scowling at her foolishness, she bent back all four flaps on the cardboard carton and began removing the newspaper packing. When her fingers struck something more solid, she carefully took out the last few papery wads to reveal a small, midnight-blue velvet box, the kind jewellers use. Only this box wasn't new. Taking a breath, she extracted the box and set it on the table. It bore no jeweller or brand name on the outside. She frowned at it as questions tumbled over themselves in her mind.

When she lifted the lid with tentative fingers, dark, blood-red gemstones glinted up at her from a bed of white satin.

Garnets?

She reached in to touch the stones, and the movement sent silver links glinting in the light.

Not loose gems ... a bracelet?

Carefully lifting it from its satiny bed, she dangled the bracelet in front of her eyes.

Garnets, no denying. Rough-cut but magnificent gems with a rich depth of colour.

She tore her gaze away from the glinting stones to once more eye the parcel's wrapping, now spread out on the table. The plain white A3 paper, sporting what appeared to be computer-generated text along with some grubby finger marks, bore her name, no mistake. But who was the giver of this surprise gift, if that's what it was? And why didn't the delivery person knock or call out? They had to come to the front door, when surely they would've heard her talking on the phone and known she was home?

She scanned the text, which listed the properties of various gemstones, and re-read the circled paragraph.

... deepening of existing love.

A thrill erupted within her, and her brows shot skyward.

Didn't Cal say something about getting me another gift? One that wouldn't run off?

Warmth flooded her soul.

He must've arranged for someone to drop the parcel here, as a surprise.

Hurrying to the back door and out onto the lawn, she dangled the bracelet from both hands and lifted it so the sun's rays caught the gems. They sparkled blood-red in the light, making her gasp.

Oh, you wonderful man! And what a wonderful surprise!

With a delighted whoop she spun on the spot into a dance of pure joy, the sparkling bracelet still dangling from her raised hands.

From its perch in a nearby gum tree, a lone magpie stopped preening to watch the performance below.

Clasping the bracelet to her chest, Libby lifted her face skyward. Then, after savouring the elation for another long moment, she opened her hand and with a reverential flourish, fastened the bracelet around her slender left wrist.

With its irregularly-shaped stones, and links and clasp more chunky than dainty, it wasn't the most delicate piece of jewellery. But it had a unique, natural beauty all its own, and suited her in a way a more delicate piece might not.

I don't love it, I adore it. It's simply stunning, and just so ... me.

Tears welling, she continued gazing at the treasured gift. 'Darling Cal,' she whispered tenderly, 'you know me better than I gave you credit for. What did I do to deserve someone like you?' Closing her eyes, she hugged her left wrist close against her chest. 'I'll never question anything you do ever again.'

13

Libby rushed to answer the phone when it rang the following evening. It'd be Cal, for sure, wanting to know what she thought of his latest gift.

But it was MJ's deep voice that responded to her animated greeting with the usual laid-back, 'Hey, Lib.'

'Oh. Hey, MJ.'

Her disappointment resonated over the phone line. At the other end of the call, MJ released a stoic breath and cleared his throat. 'Just ringin' to check ... um ... everything's okay ... with you?'

The furrow in her brow lifted. The next caller was *bound* to be Cal. Anyway, nothing could dampen her soaring spirits. 'Everything's simply *peachy*, MJ, thanks for asking. What about with you?'

'Yeah ... um ... all good.' He paused as if expecting her to say more.

She didn't. Her mind was elsewhere.

A long way elsewhere. North, at a remote mine site.

He cleared his throat again. 'So ... you're still okay for our ride tomorrow arvo?'

'Oh! The ride. Um ... sure.' Realising she must sound ungrateful, she firmed her voice. 'Looking forward to it.'

'Right-oh then. I'll ride over after lunch...?'

'Great.'

'Right. Well ... okay. I'll ... um ... see you at around one?'

'You will.' She put the phone down with a bemused grin.

MJ's still not himself, at least not with me, even when Cal's not around.

Cal.

Her expression softened and she pressed a palm against her glowing cheek.

He's probably waiting to hear from me first, doesn't want to spoil the surprise. Oh, how I love that man! He deserves a surprise too....

'Refill?' Pam Studsor hovered the teapot over Libby's half-empty cup.

'Better not.' She smiled. 'Gotta ride home after this.

Don't want to have to find a convenient bush along the way.'

Pam grinned back at her. 'Of course.' Turning to MJ, she waved the pot at him and received a silent nod in reply.

Seeing him crack what might've been a smile while Pam refilled his cup, Libby found herself once more wondering at MJ's demeanour. He'd been silent on the ride over, sitting hunched in the saddle, eyes fixed forward. As a rule he was not one for verbosity, but today he was a mere hair's breath away from mute.

One of the few times he'd spoken was when he first arrived. After nodding a greeting and laying eyes on the bracelet, he'd remarked on her new 'bling'.

The brief mention had her holding up her wrist so he could better admire the blood-red stones, and gushing about how it was another surprise gift from Cal; and didn't it suit her; and while she wasn't big on wearing jewellery this piece was worthy of an exception....

Still gushing when they set off on the ride, it took kilometres of monosyllabic responses to her questions and prompts before she realised something was wrong with MJ. But when she tried asking if he was okay, the only reply was a curt nod and a conversation-ending, 'Yep.' From that point on, an uncomfortable silence fell between them that lasted the rest of the journey.

Had he simply used up his quota of words for the day?

It was an accusation she'd thrown at him more than once when, as a tetchy teenage girl, she'd found his silences irksome. On one such occasion she'd thrown her reins at him and flounced away, leaving him holding the horses in the round yard and staring open-mouthed after her.

When her father chipped her for leaving MJ to see to their sweating mounts, she'd moaned to him about their one-sided 'chats'. This earned her a knowing grin and a droll, 'It's just the way of some cattlemen, Lib,' in response. 'They're economical with words but liberal with actions.'

Dave was certainly right about the latter point. No one knew that better than she did.

And as for the first point?

MJ's making a fine job of being 'economical with words' today.

About to tell him of the recent update from the police, and of her complaint to Will Rayner about the type of people his lax camping rules brought to the area, she decided against it. MJ clearly wasn't in the mood for conversation. And although she felt like asking why he'd invited her to join him if he didn't want her company, she let it go. The opportunity to witness her horse—another of Cal's loving gifts—working so well under saddle made the ride, and the one-sided conversation, totally worthwhile.

MJ had something on his mind, obviously, but he wasn't saying.

Fine.

'So, Libby. Am I right in thinkin' Shorty's leg's all healed?'

Doc's words brought her back to the present. She nodded. 'Hard to even spot a scar now.'

'Always was a quick healer.' Doc glanced over at the yard where the two horses stood, girths loosened, dozing in front of their partly eaten hay nets. 'Lookin' shmick too, if a bit on the chubby side.'

'Yeah, I haven't been working him much lately. Too busy with other things.' Her lips tipped into a smile. 'And your horses are all good doers.'

'It's all in the breeding, y'know.' Doc sat back with a satisfied grunt. 'His dam's a good doer, and so is the Black Flash.'

Proud as proud of his champion standardbred stallion, racing name Brian's Report, Doc was beside himself after being offered eye-watering money for the stud from powerful racing connections.

"Course I knocked back the offer,' he told MJ at the time. 'The Flash isn't for sale, now or ever. He's worth more to me here, in my stable, not only for his race wins but for his bloodline as well. Gonna use him to breed me some more youngsters,' he'd added with a wink, 'who'll "flash" past the winning posts.'

'Another Anzac bickie, Libby?' Pam waved the plate under her nose. 'Best eaten when fresh. Made them this morning, so I want them all gone by this 'arvo.'

'Y'know what else Shorty's tops at doin'?' Doc went on proudly. 'Pullin' the cart through thick bush. I take all my horses through the bush tracks 'round 'ere as part of their trainin'. Gets 'em thinkin' about where they're puttin' their feet. Some horses, they don't know what to do when they come up against a fallen log across the track. Not this little bugger,' and he hiked a thumb at the dozing Shorty.

'Without bein' told, he'd slow right down before steppin' over the obstacle, and then wait 'til he felt the wheels nudge the log, before puttin' his shoulder against the harness to tug the cart over real gentle like. Gave me a smooth ride every time, the smart little bugger.' Doc gave an indulgent chuckle. "N bein' smart, I reckon he cottoned on that it'd be an easier life being a lady's pleasure hack than a race horse, which is why he was so easy to break to the saddle. He just looked around as if to say, "Whatcha doin' up there on my back 'stead of in a cart behind me?" then gave a sort of shrug and got on with the job. Yep, that's one clever little horse.'

They stayed later than planned, finding it hard to extract themselves from the chatty Doc. By the time the two riders set off for home, the sun had dipped toward the horizon and clouds had rolled in, blocking the already weakening rays. Numerous tracks crisscrossed that section of bush, making it easy for the unwary to lose their way especially in failing light.

By silent agreement both urged their horses into a brisker walk as they traversed the darkening forest. Despite perking up while with the Studsors, MJ was, if anything, more withdrawn on the ride home. Libby scowled at his back, unable to come up with a reason she might deserve the silent treatment ... and that simply wouldn't do.

She would demand MJ tell her what was wrong.

Urging Shorty into a jog to close the gap between them she opened her mouth, only to snap it shut when MJ abruptly halted Rouge at a T-junction in the bush track.

After peering both ways, trying to see beyond the dense groves of eucalypts on either side, he mumbled without looking at her, 'I can't recognise any landmarks in this light. Do you remember if we turn right or left here?'

She craned her neck to gaze first one way and then the other. 'Not sure ... nothing looks familiar. But then I rarely come this way.' After a moment chewing her bottom lip, she brightened. 'Doc said he takes all his horses bush track training around here, so Shorty would be familiar with these paths. I bet he knows the way home.' Urging her mount forward, she loosened the reins. 'I'll give him his head and see what happens.'

MJ glanced doubtfully at her but brought Rouge in behind the gelding, who stepped out confidently once in the lead. His stride was shorter than the mare's but he needed little urging to stay ahead, making Libby grin to herself.

That's my boy, still competitive after all these years. Racing habits die hard if they ever die at all.

Dropping the reins to the pommel, she bent to put her cheek against Shorty's mane and ran her hands lovingly along both sides of his neck. Behind them, MJ eyed the tender scene from beneath his hat's pulled-down brim, saying nothing as Shorty led them along twisting paths through the shadowy bush.

Some time later he called, 'Are you sure he's taking us to your place and not Darwin?'

With a wry snort, she threw over a shoulder, 'Darwin?'

'Well, we could end up anywhere for all we—' He stopped when a shaft of light crossed his face, and a moment later the foliage parted and the horses stepped into a clearing. Up ahead MJ saw the gravel road and beyond it, glimpses of a recognisable rooftop.

The *Boronia Station* homestead.

Libby flashed him a triumphant grin. 'Yeah, we could've ended up anywhere, but we didn't.' Bending, she once more rested her cheek against the gelding's neck. 'Told you my boy'd get us home.'

'I stand correc—' MJ's breath hitched as Rouge shied violently, unseating him.

At the commotion Libby whipped her head around, to see the wild-eyed mare dart sideways into the tree line and away from whatever had startled her.

With one foot out of the stirrup, MJ slipped sideways in the saddle, bumping against the branches of a sapling before making a grab for the pommel and righting himself. An instant later, angry buzzing erupted from the large wasp nest housed in the sapling, and a squadron of insects emerged in full attack mode.

Yelling, 'Wasps! Go, GO!' Libby dug her heels into Shorty's sides.

The gelding gave a surprised grunt and leapt into a gallop, with Libby bent over his neck urging him faster. She simply held on, letting him find his own way as they flew towards the farm with MJ close behind. At a sudden bellow she glanced over her shoulder, and through the hair whipping around her face, saw MJ haul Rouge to a stop and leap from the saddle.

Oh-oh.

She brought Shorty to a sliding halt and whirled him around, to find MJ doing a wild dance on the spot, clutching at his shirt and wincing in pain.

When she shouted, 'What's wrong?' he ground out between clenched teeth, 'Got some under .... AH! ... under here,' and he began haphazardly slapping his shirt.

'Oh no.' Swinging down from the saddle, she left a snorting Shorty ground-tied and ran to MJ's side. 'Where are they?'

When the only response was another agonised, 'AH!' she clicked her tongue and stepped in to grab his shirt. As she hauled it over his head, the irately buzzing insects took off from between his shoulder blades. Libby ducked as they flew past her head, and then turned her attention to the welts forming on MJ's skin. There was a whole patch of angry-looking stings.

'Hang on, I should have some Teatree oil....' Jogging to where Shorty stood sniffing at clumps of grass, she opened a saddle bag and scratched around. 'Yeah, here it is.' Grabbing the small brown bottle, she jogged back to MJ. 'Hold still for a minute.'

Stepping behind him, she poured some of the aromatic oil into her palm and proceeded to rub it firmly across his welted, muscular back. He stood still for a moment, then shrugged her away.

She watched as he reached grimly for his shirt and dragged it over his tanned, well-built torso.

He'll make someone a gorgeous husband one day.

As she screwed the cap onto the bottle, her hand slowed.

And she'd better damn well treat him right.

14

Rolling down the car's window, Libby rested her elbow on the sill and let the warm wind blow her loose hair into a sun-bronzed brunette frenzy.

Hiring the car had been an unanticipated expense but worth every cent for the eight-hour trek to the mine site, over three hundred and fifty kilometres inland of Geraldton. It wasn't good to break down anywhere, but the isolated Great Northern Highway to Mount Magnet would be worse than most, especially for a young woman travelling alone. And the ute had been warning her for some time it was more than likely to let her down.

While she could've swapped cars with her folks, they'd be sure to object to her driving so far on her own, and maybe spoil the surprise by alerting Cal. Better to tell them after she was safely back home on the farm. What was the saying in corporate circles? Better to beg forgiveness than approval? Something like that, anyway. And Harry's sale had boosted the farm's coffers, so why not use a small portion of the money on something that made her heart glad?

She gave a joyous shiver of anticipation, imagining Cal's initially stunned and then elated greeting at her unannounced arrival. That alone would make the trip worth every minute of 'white line fever'.

Hoping she'd correctly interpreted the most recent shift roster he'd sent by email, she pictured the two of them spending his days off sleeping in each morning and later, enjoying tours of the Mount Magnet area.

A hike up Warramboo Hill could be on the cards, along with a picnic lunch in the deserted gold rush township of Lennonville on the tourist trail. It might be fun to meet some of his workmates too, but she wanted Cal to herself for most of the time.

That was the whole purpose of the trip, a surprise 'gift' of her company. A gift they could both relish.

She glanced at the clock on the SUV's dash and then at the fuel gauge.

Only a few kilometres to Dalwallinu, roughly the halfway point in the journey, where she'd top up the car's tank as well as her own. A hot coffee and meat pie sure would be welcome after four hundred-odd kilometres of tepid water, biscuits, and fruit. She wouldn't linger, though.

In just over another three hundred kilometres she'd be falling into Cal's open arms.

I'll be with you soon, babe.

The alarm once more blared its unwelcome message, this time mid-afternoon.

Cal inhaled and blinked his eyes open, resisting the impulse to straightaway close them again. He hated the earlies, but night shifts were the real killers. While he'd catch some sleep during the day, he had to be careful not to sleep too long, otherwise he'd spend the next night lying wide awake.

Rubbing his eyes, he made to rise. Feeling the slight weight on his chest, he paused and smiled.

She'd surprised him by being there when he got back to the unit after end of shift.

Gently lifting the slender limb, he tucked it beside her sleeping form. Sprawled on top of the rumpled bedclothes beside him, she was all satiny skin over taut body, topped with a mane of hair that smelled like ripe peaches.

Taking care not to disturb her, he sat up with an indulgent sigh.

She's prepared to put up with my shifts, and all my comings and goings. I'm a lucky man.

Slipping out of bed, he padded to the bathroom. Pausing in the doorway he once more eyed the curvaceous shape on the bed, his lips stretching into a self-satisfied grin.

A lucky man indeed....

As he disappeared into the bathroom, the figure on the bed moved, gave a soft groan, and raised her tousled blonde head.

Dalwallinu's Country Muncher Cafe buzzed with moleskin-clad locals, tee-shirted tourists, caravan-creased grey nomads, and what felt like hordes of sticky black flies. The country music crackling from speakers mounted on the ceiling was hard to hear over the babble of voices.

The sheer number of bodies, combined with aromatic heat from pie warmers, hotplates, deep fryers, and the overworked coffee machine, rendered the building's interior too warm for the single, chugging air conditioner to handle.

Wiping the sweat from her top lip, Libby glanced around at the full tables.

Oh well, having a takeaway in the car would likely be cooler, and have me on my way again sooner.

She joined the queue at the counter, just another customer doing the fly-chasing 'salute' while stretching her back and rolling her neck, waiting for her turn to order.

With the staff on no-rush 'outback time' it took a while,

but finally the round, fifty-something woman behind the counter asked without looking up, 'What'll it be?'

'A flat white please, and a plain meat pie.' Just saying the words had Libby's mouth watering.

'That's a pie-'n-coffee, comin' right up.' Absently waving flies from her face, the woman lifted her head to eye the attractive young woman standing before her. 'Anythin' else?'

'That's all, thanks.'

'On your own, love?' At Libby's nod, the waitress gave a frazzled smile. 'Where you from?'

'Down south.'

'Headin' to the mine?'

Another nod.

'Thought as much. That's where most young'uns are headin' when they come through 'ere.' A motherly expression settled on her sweating, florid face. 'Best watch yourself up there, love. Miners can be a rough bunch, and some don't wanna take no for an answer. Good-lookin' girl like you could end up in a bunch of trouble through no fault of 'er own, just by bein' there.'

Libby smiled. 'Thanks for the warning, but I'll only be on site a few days....'

'The buggers won't take long to sniff you out.'

'... and I'm joining my partner up there. He works at the mine.'

'Oh, right. Well then, you should be okay ... if he takes care of you proper-like.' The woman was already eyeing the next customer in the queue. 'Find yourself a chair if you can, love, 'n I'll bring your order when it's ready.'

'Thanks, but I'd prefer takeaway.'

'Right you are. Now, who's next?'

'Libby? What the *hell?'* From where he stood in the partly open doorway of his above-ground, transportable accommodation unit called a 'donga', a heart-poundingly bare chested Cal stared down at her, his expression nothing like what she'd expected.

Instead of surprised and elated, he looked more ... alarmed, indignant ... *embarrassed?*

'Surprise!' She tried for a jubilant tone but her treacherous voice wobbled. Where was the ecstatic, open-arms greeting? The scene wasn't playing out at all the way she'd imagined.

Dragging fingers through his uncombed hair, he glanced over a shoulder and pulled the door closed behind him before stepping onto the small landing. 'What are you doing here?'

'I thought it would be a nice surprise—'

'To spring a visit on me?'

Was that *accusation* in his tone? 'For us to ... spend your days off together.' A crease formed in her brow and her lips lost their upward tilt. 'Aren't you glad to see me?'

'Glad?' His voice trailed off as his gaze flicked to the closed door again.

The furrow in her brow deepened as she watched him struggling for words. 'Cal?'

'What?' Turning, he dropped his chin to his chest. 'Oh ... yes. Yes, of course I'm glad to see you, Lib.' He rubbed his right ear and then his nose. 'It's just ... I never expected to see you *here*.'

She managed a tremulous grin. 'That *is* the whole idea of a surprise. Like how you surprised me with that lovely gift.'

He lifted his head but still wouldn't meet her eyes. 'Oh yeah, the horse.'

Jingling the bracelet on her arm, she made to raise it. 'No, I mean—'

'Look, Lib.'

At his pained expression and abrupt words, she lowered her arm again.

'My donga,' and he jerked a thumb toward the closed door behind him, 'is a bit of a mess. A right pig sty in fact. And I've just got out of the shower. How about you give me a few minutes to sort myself out. You can grab a coffee at the camp wet mess.' He glanced at his watch. 'Or a glass of wine if you prefer. It's after four, so the bar should be open.'

Pointing to a sizeable building in the centre of the single men's accommodation units, he said dismissively, 'I'll join you there. Won't be long.'

He hadn't given her a hello kiss, or even a hug. Hadn't made any move to touch her, in fact.

'O...kay.' Frowning, she backed down from the landing. 'So I'll wait there for you?' At his nod she turned away. Hearing the door open and quickly close again behind her, she glanced over a shoulder. Cal was gone.

Well, that didn't exactly go to plan.

Her chest tightened and her mind raced as she trudged toward the barn-like mess. Its double doors were latched open, and inside only a few of the tables had people sitting at them.

All men.

And all staring at her.

Their unapologetic gawping had her own gaze bouncing from spot to spot, until her eyes fell on the servery. Seeing a woman behind the counter, she made for it with a sense of relief. After ordering a coffee from the dull-eyed, clearly jaded waitress, she risked a peek over a shoulder to find most of the other clientele had lost interest in her. Releasing a breath, she swept a glance around the eatery and spotted a table tucked in a corner a healthy distance from the others.

The perfect spot for a quiet word with Cal. After coming all this way to surprise him, I need to know why it feels like I've done something wrong.

Coffee in hand, she strode to the table and sank into one of the chairs. After removing the lid from the takeaway cup she took a sip and pulled a face. Obviously instant, it wasn't a patch on the espresso coffee from the Country Muncher cafe. She shoved the lid back on and pushed the cup away.

'Whassup, darlin'?' a greasy voice asked. 'Mess coffee not to your likin'?'

Two men approached the table, accompanied by a strange, though not entirely unfamiliar smoky smell—she'd been to her share of teenage parties—underpinned with the rancid stench of body odour. Both wore predatory expressions, while the taller of the two also had weird eyes and a habit of flicking his tongue in and out like a lizard. And was it her imagination or was his tongue split, like a snake's?

Knots formed in her already tense stomach.

'Mind if we join you?' the first man enquired, hands already grasping the back of a chair.

'Well, I—'

''Course she don't mind,' the lizard man wheezed. He proceeded to flip a chair around and perch himself on it, resting heavily tattooed arms over the backrest. 'Sittin' here all alone she'd be glad of the company, wouldn't ya love.' It wasn't a question.

Having flopped into the other chair, the first man sat forward to rest his elbows on the table. 'Haven't seen you here before, pretty lady.' He stared into her face, running his tongue over his lips in a way that made her skin crawl. 'You new to site?'

Clasping her coffee cup in treacherously clammy

hands, she pulled it closer as if for protection. Sitting straighter, she said with more bravado than she felt, 'I'm meeting my boyfriend. He's on his way here now.'

Lizard man's tongue flicked out and in, out and in. 'Boyfriend, hey?' When he ran his creepy eyes over her, she cringed and looked away.

'What's 'is name then, this boyfriend of yours?' the first man asked.

'Cal.' Swallowing, she said more firmly, 'Callum McDougall.'

Both men chorused, 'Oh-hoh!' and rocked back in their chairs, smirking at each other.

'Another of the Tom Cat's conquests, are ya?' Leaning in, the first man peered more closely at her tanned face and neck, checked shirt, and the short fingernails of her slender, work-hardened hands. 'Or ... could it be you're his little woman, from down on the farm?'

When she merely frowned, the lizard man wheezed, 'Reckon you're right, Rod. This here's the little woman, venturing off the farm to come visit lover boy at work.'

'Yeah, Snake. Reckon I've picked it.' He wiped a grimy hand down his shirt and extended it. 'But where are our manners? This here's Snake, and I'm Rod—'

'*Hot* Rod,' Snake interjected with a suggestive wink.

'We're Casanova's ... er ... Cal's mates.' Rod's taunting gaze flicked to her chest, and stayed there.

Libby shuddered and kept her hands clasped in her lap,

resisting the urge to fasten her top button and check all the others were still done up.

Why had she taken the chair that backed against the wall? It meant she was penned in, unable to escape the skin-crawling advances of Cal's so-called 'mates'. That, teamed with the chilly reception from Cal himself, left her wishing she hadn't 'ventured' off the farm at all.

Wishing wholeheartedly she was back there right now.

15

When Cal's gaze fell on the three at the table, the two leering men and an ashen-faced Libby, he shouted, 'Hey!' and quickened his pace. Marching over, he glowered at the two men and demanded, 'Whad'ya think you're doing?'

Both men sat back in their chairs grinning. 'Just keepin' this pretty lady company,' Rod said greasily, 'while she waits for her boyfriend. Oh, hang on. That's you, ain't it?'

Stepping up to shove the man sideways, Cal growled, 'Get lost. Both of you.'

'Now, now.' Rod straightened and raised his hands, palms forward. 'Don't get your knickers in a twist. We're leavin', ain't we, Snake?'

Already on his feet, Snake was staring at Cal through

narrowed lizard eyes. After a quick glance Cal ignored him, while taking care to keep his distance.

'Far be it from us to linger where we're not wanted,' Rod went on, languidly rising from his chair and dusting off his pants, 'and meddle with *affairs* of the heart.'

His emphasis on the word 'affairs' wasn't lost on Cal. His expression darkened further, but he remained silent.

One side of Rod's top lip twisted upwards and he gave a dismissive grunt. 'Let's go, Snake, 'n leave these two lovebirds to their coffees.' Throwing Cal a wink as they moved off he said affably, 'Have fun you two. Catch you later, mate.'

Libby watched them saunter away before fixing questioning eyes on Cal. He didn't meet her gaze, instead keeping his head bent as he pulled out a chair and sat.

'Cal?' At the indignation in her tone, he met her eyes briefly before his gaze slipped away to rove the room.

'Don't worry about them, Lib, they're just *idiots*.' The last word came out like a snarl.

She frowned. 'What's going on, Cal?'

'Nothing.' He cleared his throat. 'Nothing's "going on". They're just messing with you. They do that to everyone. Just ignore them.'

'They seemed to assume I was another of your ... conquests?'

His released breath whooshed from between tight lips. 'I told you, those idiots get off on messing with people. And if you let them get under your skin, you're an idiot too.'

Libby's head jerked and she stared at him, affronted. 'Did you just call me an idiot?'

After muttering something under his breath, Cal raised his eyes to meet hers. 'Sorry, Lib. I....'

'You what?'

'I ... guess I've ... spent too much time around blokes like them.'

'And it's turning you into a bastard too?'

He blinked and released another aggravated breath. 'Spose I deserve that.'

'No "suppose" about it.' Sitting back, she crossed her arms. 'And after coming all this way to spend time with you, only to be treated like an unwelcome pest and then accosted by your loser mates—'

'They're not my mates—'

'—I think I deserve an explanation.'

'Look, I told you those idiots were just messing with you—with us both—and I've apologised for acting like a mongrel. And if I made you feel like a pest ... sorry.'

She crossed her arms tighter and continued glaring at him.

'I also told you—' At her expression he said quickly, 'I *suggested* you ignore those idiots. What more do you want from me?'

'Surely you can understand how I'm feeling right now?' Uncrossing her arms, she sat forward to fix him with an intense gaze. 'Having been given the brush-off by my boyfriend, who I came all this way to be with, and then taunted with sick insinuations from his supposed mates?'

'*Again,* they're no mates of mine, and I *didn't* brush you off—'

'No kiss, hug, or even a smile when I arrived? Keeping me standing outside before sending me here,' and she indicated the mess hall with a derogatory sweep of an arm, 'to wait for you like some pathetic ... groupie?' Her voice rose. '*That's* your idea of a loving greeting?'

He flapped a hand at her. 'Keep your voice down. There's enough gossip circling around here without you adding to it.'

'*Me?* What about you, Mr "Tom Cat Casanova", or whatever they call you. What's that about, by the way?'

'Like I said, they're just yanking your chain.' Raking fingers through his hair, he said resignedly, 'I'm sorry about all this, babe. You just ... caught me off-guard.' At her unconvinced shrug his expression hardened. 'But this is a work camp, not somewhere you can expect a warm reception when you simply,' and he flicked out up-turned palms, 'turn up unannounced. Otherwise you can expect the likes of Rod and Snake as a welcoming committee.'

She released a breath and slumped back in her chair. 'You're right, this was a bad idea.'

Cal eyed her intently and then reached across to take her hands in his. 'And ... I have to tell you....'

She gave a long blink and sat forward. 'May as well get it over with.'

'These aren't my days off. Tonight I'm on the ... first ... of two night shifts.'

It was actually the second of two, but if she knew that she might want to stay. He recalled Alinta's affronted expression when he'd hastily ushered her from his donga. No, it wouldn't do for Libby to stay. Wouldn't do at all.

Tugging her hands out of his grasp, she gaped at him. 'So I've come all this way only to have you working the nights and sleeping during the days?'

'I'm sorry, babe—'

'You're sorry? What for this time? Let me guess. Could it be for not giving me your new roster details so I don't make an eight hundred kilometre journey for *nothing?*' She slammed an open hand on the table and leaned forward. 'How *could* you, Cal.'

'Hey, it was your choice to spring a visit on me. I never suggested it.'

'*Spring* a visit on you? *That's* how you see this?' Her shoulders sagged and she slumped back again, once more crossing her arms.

They sat without speaking for long, tense moments, both facing away.

Libby broke the silence but kept her eyes downcast as she said slowly, 'This was supposed to be my gift to you, a lovely, romantic surprise. A gift for both of us really, 'cos I was *so* looking forward to spending a few precious days with you.'

She smiled sadly to herself. 'I drove up in a hire car and

thought we could use it to do some sightseeing, even picked out some local places of interest. And I was going to talk to you while we travelled around, about the farm and other stuff I can't tell anyone else.'

Cal finally looked at her. 'Stuff? Like what?'

'Oh,' and she gave a bitter laugh, 'I won't bother you with it now.'

He blew a long breath. 'Well ... we'd may as well have a chat at least, as you've come all this way.'

'Yeah ... I guess so.' She gave a resigned sigh. 'So, you recall the incident with Harry, how I reported it to the police?'

'I remember.'

'The local sergeant called at the farm the other day. Turns out they suspect a group of young thugs camping at Will Rayner's place of injuring Harry.'

'What d'ya know, the cops have actually done something. So they've charged the young wankers?'

She gave a cynical huff. 'Apparently they have insufficient evidence to lay any charges. And according to the sergeant, they're not able to take any further action in the case.'

'Another fail by the constabulary.' Cal frowned. 'That sucks.'

'It does, especially as this same group is suspected of other crimes around the district, including the recent fire.'

When he gave an amused snort and mumbled, 'The

cops'll struggle to pin that one on 'em,' Libby frowned at him. 'Why do you say that?'

His only answer was an awkward shifting in his seat.

Her frown deepened. 'Wait ... do you know something about who was responsible for lighting that fire?'

'What? No.' He rubbed his ear and nose.

'Because if you did,' she said slowly, still studying his face, 'you would've given the information to the police?'

'That's right. 'Course I would've.'

'So why'd you say what you did?'

'Just thinking aloud—'

'So share your thoughts. I'd like to hear them.'

After straightening in his chair, shifting forward in the seat and then back again, he said, 'Well ... I ... figured if they can't nick'em for the attack on Harry, it's ... unlikely the cops'll nick'em for the fire either.'

'That's what you were thinking?'

He nodded.

'That and nothing else?'

Another tight-lipped nod.

The crease in her brow remained firmly in place as she continued studying him.

'So,' he asked cautiously, 'that's it for Harry's case?'

'Seems that way. Though I did alert Rayner to the fact he was harbouring criminals.'

'You sure that was a good idea? It might come back to bite you.'

'He needed to know. And anyway, he shouldn't be—'

At the loud chime from her mobile they both gave a start.

Muttering, 'Damn,' she dug the phone out of a pocket and checked the screen.

SORRY ABOUT THIS, the all-capitals text read, BUT THERE'S BEEN AN INCIDENT AT THE FARM. CALL ME WHEN YOU GET THIS. It was signed MJ.

Libby sprang to her feet. 'Something's happened on the farm.' Pausing, she studied Cal's face and recalled the scene of her rather disastrous arrival. 'I should head back there.'

'You're leaving? Now?'

Catching the note of relief in his voice, she said brusquely, 'Yes, now. I'll phone MJ from the car to get the details of what's happened.'

'It's late in the day to set off on a long drive.' He said it carefully, as though worried how she'd take it. And there was no insistence she stay the night and leave in the morning.

'I may as well go,' she snapped, 'you'll be at work all night anyway. And it's unlikely I'd get much sleep in any case, fretting over what's happening at home.'

'What if you get drowsy on the road?'

'I'll pull over for a nap. It'll be fine, don't worry.' She stopped herself from adding, 'If you *care* enough to worry,' instead staring silently at him for another beat.

Averting his gaze, he murmured, 'Well, okay then. Drive safe, babe.'

That's it? That's all you have to say to me?

'Oh, and you don't need to worry I might "spring" another visit on you,' she said caustically. 'I've learned my lesson.' Turning on her heel, she strode away, giving him a back-handed wave when he called after her, 'Bye, Lib.'

16

W hat a disaster.

  After spending the first hundred kilometres angry, resentful, and disappointed, Libby was now deflated, sad, and anxious.

So much for the anticipated enthusiastic greeting and days of one-on-one time together, sightseeing and picnicking. Nothing worked out the way I'd hoped. And here I am, barely an hour later, rushing back home. Worse still, MJ's not answering his phone.

Without meaning to, she pressed harder on the accelerator.

I have no idea what's happened down there ... and may still be happening.

She yawned, blinked, and glanced at the fuel gauge.

Hopefully there's an all-hours servo open when I get to Dalwallinu. Please let it be one that offers hot, drinkable coffee.

When her thoughts returned to the ill-fated visit with Cal, she shoved the images to the back of her mind. If she examined them too closely she'd fret, and right now there was no point fretting. She had a long drive ahead of her, and an 'incident' of some kind awaiting her at home.

Keeping hold of the steering wheel, she waggled her fingers to stretch them and settled herself more comfortably in the driver's seat.

Yep, a long way to go and nobody with me to share the driving.

It was after eight pm by the time she motored into Dalwallinu. The town was ominously quiet, with a timber, colonial-styled country pub the only well-lit business in the main street. Slowing as she passed the Country Muncher cafe—was it really only hours earlier she'd called in there?—she peered into the dimly lit building.

Closed.

Damn.

As was the nearby service station.

Double damn.

Unsure what else to do, she pulled into a parking bay in front of the pub.

Someone in here might know of another servo. And I may as well get something to eat, and try ringing MJ again.

With a groan, she climbed from the car and took a moment to shake out her legs and feet to revive the circulation. Stretching her arms above her head, she raised her face to the sky and was greeted with a blanket of stars. The night air was soft on her skin and still slightly warm, and in the distance a curlew gave a mournful cry.

If she didn't have so much on her mind she would've enjoyed being here, in the middle of nowhere.

Dropping her arms to her sides, she took care to lock the car before heading to the pub. The way her luck was going, she'd be likely to come out and find the car gone and herself stranded.

Making her way between the painted timber posts and under the top storey's veranda, she was almost at the pub's latched-back doors when her mobile chimed with a call. Moving to one side, she checked the screen for the caller ID and immediately accepted the call.

'At last! I've been trying to ring you—'

'Yeah, sorry Lib. I left my mobile in the car.' MJ's deep voice rumbled from her phone's speaker. 'Things have been a bit ... crazy here.'

'So what's happened?'

'Firstly, the situation's under control so you don't need to panic. Secondly, where are you calling from?'

'Dalwallinu. I've stopped for fuel and dinner.'

'So you're on your way home?'

'Yep.'

'Dalwallinu's around halfway isn't it?'

'Roughly. You know the area?'

'No, I just ... looked up your route on the map.'

'Oh.' Her forehead wrinkled. 'Too much time on your hands?'

'Something like that,' he said hastily. 'Anyway, I had hoped to talk to you before you set off.'

'Well I couldn't reach you, so thought I'd better hit the road.'

'Alone?'

'Yep.'

He blew a concerned breath. 'I thought Cal might....'

'Come with me?' She gave a snort. 'You thought wrong.'

'He knew why you were rushing back?'

'He did.'

'And still he let you drive all the way in the dark?' There was no disguising the condemnation in MJ's voice.

'Forget Cal,' she said brusquely, 'and stop stalling. Tell me what's happened.'

'Well, like I said, there's no need to panic, but....' There was reluctance and apology in MJ's voice. 'We had a bad storm, and your place copped a lightning strike.'

She gasped. 'What was hit?'

'The hayshed.'

'Oh no....'

'And ... most of your hay was lost, either burned or soaked by the fire fighters. Of course they had no choice—'

'My whole hay store, gone?'

'Pretty much.'

Moaning, 'No, no,' she squeezed her eyes shut and pressed fingers to her temples.

At the other end of the call, MJ's wince deepened. This wasn't the time to tell her the whole story, not when she still had a long way to drive ... alone. 'Things are under control here now, so there's no need for you to rush home. Why not overnight there and finish the trip tomorrow?'

'But....' Picturing the fuel gauge on the hire car and the closed service station, she blinked tired, scratchy eyes. 'Well, I ... guess I *could* do that. If you're sure—'

'There's nothing that can't wait 'til tomorrow.'

'Anything else I should know?'

He chose his words carefully. 'Plenty of time tomorrow to go over the details. What time should I expect you?'

'I'll set off at first light, so should be there by late morning.' She raised her eyes to take in the pub. 'That's assuming I can find a room for the night. If not, I could be home in four hours or thereabouts.'

'Dalwallinu's not exactly high on the tourist must-visit list. There's bound to be a room at the pub.'

'I'm about to find that out.'

'And if you do end up driving home tonight—and it'd be better if you don't—let me know so I can keep an eye out.'

'Alright.'

'But I won't expect to see you 'til the morning.'

'Okay. And thanks MJ.'

'Take care, Lib.'

. . .

'All the units are taken,' the blue-rinsed publican behind the bar said in a cracked, smoky voice, 'but I can give'ya a room upstairs.' She lifted her chin toward the impressive timber staircase that led to the upper floor. Its carved red cedar base effectively split the downstairs area into public bar and dining room.

Libby had glimpsed the 'units' on her way in. Despite yearning for a hot shower and clean bed to stretch out on and close her eyes, she was secretly glad none of the low-roofed, metal-clad transportable buildings was available. While solid enough, they appeared soulless, and had mine vehicles and spotlight-bedecked cowboy utes parked in front of them. If the interior walls were as thin as she envisaged, it was likely she'd be kept awake by occupants of the units either side.

Even if the noise from downstairs filtered upward, at least the rooms inside the historic timber hotel would have some character, judging by the dado-lined dining room with carved Victorian dresser and open fireplace. And the noise level was already dropping as more diners, replete after what looked like man-sized roast-of-the-day meals and slabs of apple pie with ice cream, left for the evening.

Sensing someone come to stand beside her, she swivelled to see the motherly waitress from the cafe smiling at her.

The woman nudged her with an elbow. 'Back so soon?'

At Libby's reluctant head dip, she asked quietly, 'Things didn't turn out like you planned, love?'

Another slow nod.

'That bloke of yours didn't take care of you like he should've, hey?' The woman patted her on the arm and then fixed the publican with a steely glance. 'Look after this one, Val. How 'bout you give 'er the honeymoon suite?'

A *honeymoon* suite? The ache Libby had been ignoring rose grindingly to the surface. Going by Cal's chilly greeting earlier, their need for accommodation like that might be a distant dream. She blinked, swallowed, and raised a hand. 'I don't expect—'

With her gaze fixed on the publican, the woman waved away Libby's objection. 'Come on, Val. Us girls gotta stick together, 'n I reckon this girl's had somethin' of a hard time, not to mention come a long way on 'er own. Reckon she could use a sound sleep in a comfy bed.'

Val frowned uncertainly. 'I have other rooms....'

'Which will do just—'

The woman squeezed Libby's arm to silence her and continued addressing the publican. 'As far as honeymoon suites go yours isn't exactly top of the wazza, Val, but it's the best you got and the quietest in the whole place. Got its own bathroom too. And it's not like there'd be many takers for that particular room tonight.' She swept an arm around the few, high-viz wearing patrons still in the dining room, and gave an amused snort.

Val stared at her for another moment. Then, with a

sniff, she reached for a key from the cabinet behind her. 'That'll be one-twenty for the night. Breakfast is extra. Sign here.' She pushed a form and pen in front of Libby.

Beside her, the motherly woman slapped a hand on the bar. 'There y'go, love. Got y'self a quiet room to get a good night's sleep. I'm bettin' you'll feel like a new woman in the mornin'.'

Managing to smile warmly at her, Libby murmured, 'Thanks so much—' She frowned. 'Sorry, I don't even know your name?'

'Fay.'

'Nice to meet you, Fay. I'm Libby.'

'Good to meet you too, 'n no need to thank me. Was just doin' what any good country woman would do for another.' Fay gave Libby's arm a final pat. 'You take care, okay?' With a brisk nod, she went to join the long-suffering man waiting for her by the door.

After signing and paying for the room, Libby carried her overnight bag up the staircase and along the corridor, checking room numbers as she went. Stopping outside a solid, lead-lighted timber door at the end of the corridor, she double-checked the room number before taking out the heavy key Val had given her and slipping it into the lock. When she pushed it open, the door gave a creak of aged hinges.

Leaning in, she swept a glance over her 'home' for the night.

On the outside-facing wall, French doors with tastefully

etched glass panels opened onto the front veranda and allowed filtered light into the room. The most eye-catching feature, however, was the tall, ornate iron bed, whose polished brass head and base sported elegant metal scrolls in heart shapes of varying sizes. Hearts were definitely the room's theme for they also featured, in an understated rather than tacky way, in the surprisingly elegant bed linen.

Through a partly open side door Libby glimpsed a bathroom with period fittings, including a claw foot bathtub. Beside it, a dark-timbered, colonial-styled vanity unit housed white towels in its open side shelves and a selection of upmarket toiletries on its marble counter top.

Libby released a long, grateful breath.

I SO need this.

Soaking away the external, and more importantly internal, grime of the day with a glass of bubbles in hand? Oh yes.

Why not spoil myself a little, to make up for....

When the inner ache rose again, she inhaled deeply and stuck out her chin. It didn't pay to dwell on the day's events, she simply had to toughen up and get home.

And as for spoiling myself, I reckon Cal can reimburse me for at least some of the cost of this trip. He owes me that much at least.

Her dinner, lamb roast of the day with lashings of vegetables and Vegemite-flavoured gravy—a forgotten favourite she would now be revisiting at home—and accompanied by a glass of wine, arrived while she was unpacking. She tucked hungrily into the food but kept the wine aside to have while soaking in the tub.

And that little indulgence was even better than she'd imagined.

Among the toiletries provided, she found a heart-shaped glass jar of 'Botanicals for Two' bath salts. Ignoring the 'two' she scattered the entire contents over the filling tub, inhaling the floral fragrance as she finished undressing. With one hand holding the champagne flute well clear, she slipped into the warm water.

Now I'm going to relax and not let myself worry about anything. Like MJ said, plenty of time for that tomorrow....

Despite telling herself that over and over, it took Libby a while to drop off to sleep after finishing her soak in the bath, putting on the lacy chemise she'd bought specially for the trip, and climbing onto the tall bed. She snuggled beneath the covers and closed her heavy eyelids, only to see again Cal's expression when he'd opened his door to her knock.

There'd been surprise in his eyes, naturally, but flashes of other things too. Alarm? Resentment? *Guilt?*

Blowing a tense, exasperated breath she rolled over, only to hear a replay of his words, '*Libby?* What the *hell* are you doing here?' Where was the beaming smile and joyous, 'Babe? Is that you?'

Why a frosty chill instead of the warm hugs and

lingering kisses he would've got if their roles were reversed? If anything, he'd seemed ... unhappy to see her.

Unhappy?

Since they'd been together, she'd always felt somehow responsible for making and keeping Cal happy. Like the day she caught him scowling into the mirror while fingering newly formed wrinkles on his forehead. Hastening to assure him that any signs of ageing only made her cherish him more, and that she looked forward to their growing old together, she'd been crestfallen when he appeared more offended than reassured by her words.

She gave herself a mental shake and refocused on the now.

Was she being overly sensitive, or had there really been accusation in his tone when he talked of her having 'sprung a visit' on him? On top of that there was the change to his roster, which he hadn't bothered to tell her about.

But the thought that kept coming back to her, and what hurt most of all, was that despite the weeks they'd spent apart, he *clearly* wasn't glad to see her on his front doorstep.

She was still frowning when sleep finally claimed her some time later.

The following morning she was woken by a discreet tap on the door, followed by a soft thump on the carpeted corridor floor. After allowing herself a languorous stretch in the roomy bed, she climbed down and padded to the door.

On a heart-shaped tray outside, a glass of juice sat beside a bowl of fresh fruit, along with the makings of a pot of tea, a plate under a metal cover, slices of toast in a chrome toast rack, and a bowl containing individually wrapped butters and condiments.

When she lifted the metal cover the warm aroma of bacon and eggs wafted upward, making her mouth water.

This'll keep me going 'til I get home.

At the thought of what awaited her at the farm, her stomach gave an apprehensive flip.

Yet another disaster to deal with. Will they never end?

17

He was waiting for her when she pulled in at the farm, sitting on the front veranda hugging his knees and looking grim. And was that a dressing on his right arm?

Oh-oh....

She didn't bother putting the ute in the shed, instead parking right there and jumping out. As she strode up to him MJ rose to his feet, dusting off his cargo pants.

'Lib.'

'MJ.'

'How was the drive?'

'Fine.' She answered distractedly, her gaze drawn to the front door. 'What the—?'

'Yeah.' MJ took a deep breath. 'The house was broken into during the storm.'

'*Broken into?*' She flicked him an accusing glance. 'You didn't say anything about that on the phone!'

'Didn't want you to panic and do somethin' foolish, like drive all the way without stoppin'.'

She was barely listening, eyeing the splintered door frame and swearing under her breath. After hurrying to the door and fisting it open, she peered apprehensively inside.

The lighter pieces of furniture in the living area had been flipped over and some flung around the room, and the contents of her CD and DVD racks were strewn across the floor. The window blind had been torn down and lay amid pieces of a broken table lamp. Next to it, a smashed photo frame held a cherished family photo—a beaming Dave and Rhonda at a district gymkhana, standing with Libby and a blue-ribboned Biddy, her first horse.

With a distraught glance at MJ, who nodded it was safe to enter, she stepped over the debris and made her way to the kitchen.

This room had fared worse than the living area, with smashed crockery, dented pots and pans and pantry contents littering the counter, table, and floor. Everything was covered in a dusting of flour from the opened container which lay on its side amid the rubble.

Libby turned dismayed, incredulous eyes on MJ.

'Yeah, it's a right mess,' he said quietly, 'but only in these two rooms. The others are fine, I checked.' He looked away, recalling the lingering scent of her in her bedroom.

'Have you seen Sam since this happened?' Her voice rose a notch. 'Is he okay?'

MJ nodded. 'Probably slept through the whole thing. Found him in one of the feed bins sleepin' off a big meal of baby mice.'

She blew a puff of air through pursed lips.

'You'll need to check if anything was taken and let the cops know,' he went on. 'Reckon I disturbed the no-good delinquents before they could finish the job, so I'm hopin' they didn't get around to pinchin' anything. The gutless wonders took off soon as they heard me yellin'.'

When he absently rubbed the dressing on his arm, she remembered and stared at it in concern. 'What happened?'

'Oh, that. It's nothin' really. Just got a bit burnt fighting the fire.'

'Fire? You mean ... in my hayshed?' Her stomach fell further at the reminder she had other destruction to inspect.

He nodded. 'When I spotted the smoke I alerted the firies and came straight here. Luckily you have that water outlet and hose by the shed. I used it to start fightin' the blaze.'

'Oh MJ! When I asked you to keep an eye on the place while I was away, I never expected you to....' Her voice trailed off and she stared at him, aghast.

'There's no way you could've anticipated any of this.'

'No, but....' She swallowed and indicated his bandaged arm with a lift of her chin. 'How bad is the injury?'

'Just a small patch of second degree burns. Looks worse than it is 'cos of all the bandaging the medics insisted on applying.'

Once more murmuring, 'Oh, MJ,' she moved closer and took his arm in both hands. At his sudden, audible intake of breath, she raised her eyes to meet his. What she saw in them had her snatching back her hands, taking a hasty step away, and staring wide-eyed at him before frowning and averting her gaze.

The way he looked at her!

What was going on?

Was she missing something?

A tense silence fell, broken only by the carolling of a nearby magpie.

Finally, MJ cleared his throat and spoke. 'Yeah ... um ... as far as the break-in goes, I reckon the same crims that injured Harry came back for another go.'

After forcing her focus to the strewn debris again, she muttered darkly, 'Getting back at me, probably.'

'Getting back at you? For what?'

'Dobbing them in to Rayner. They were camping at his place, and I guess he must've chucked them out after I told him what they'd been up to.'

MJ winced. 'Yeah ... dobbing people in often brings consequences for the dobber.'

'*Dobber?* Well, thank you *very* much.' Eyes blazing, she snapped, 'And what are you saying?' Anger was safer ground. 'That I brought this on myself?'

'No, of course not. Just ... these types tend to exact revenge when someone has the guts to push back.'

This time Libby broke the strained silence. 'You're right. Sorry, I—'

'No need to apologise.' He indicated the damaged room with a sweep of his uninjured arm. 'You've had a bad shock.'

'Which I had no right to take out on you, when I should be thanking you for seeing off delinquents, fighting a fire, and getting yourself injured in the process.' Sagging into a nearby chair, she cupped her face in her hands and muttered, 'There I was thinking I'd had my share of disasters for the time being.'

Wishing he could do more to comfort her, he said gruffly, 'No need to thank me. Just doin' what any neighbour would.'

Where had she heard those words or similar recently? Oh yeah, from the helpful Fay in Dalwallinu, where Libby had once more been forced to rely on the kindness of strangers. She grimaced beneath her hands.

'So,' MJ went on, 'what are you going to do?'

Blowing a resigned breath, she lifted her head. 'Report the break-in to the police, I guess, and then clean up this mess.'

'I alerted the cops when it happened. They've already been to inspect the damage.'

'Really? Well, thanks MJ.' She flashed him a weary but

grateful glance. ''Spose I'd better inspect the hayshed too, before starting on the clean-up in here.'

She looked so miserable his heart rose in his throat. Surely there was something more he could do? 'Can I get you something first? Cup of tea maybe?' At her dispirited head shake he pressed, 'You must be thirsty after the long trip.'

'Yeah, but I can't trust any of that,' and she indicated the debris-strewn kitchen. 'Will have to buy all new supplies.'

Even as she spoke MJ was reaching into his pocket. Extracting two English Breakfast tea bags, which he knew to be her favourite, he waved them in front of her. 'Brought these from home.'

'Oh, you angel.' She managed a wan smile. 'At least the water won't be contaminated.'

'And your kettle's undamaged, and we can clean up a few cups.'

'That's something, I guess.' She watched him forge a path through the wreckage to the sink, where he filled the kettle and got it going. Rising to her feet, Libby cleared an area, righted the overturned chairs, and set them up at the table, using her sleeve to wipe away the coatings of flour.

'So,' he said casually, 'how was Cal doing?'

'Cal?' She couldn't keep the bitter edge from her voice. 'Oh, he's just *fine.*'

MJ paused to glance at her with raised brows. 'Shame you had to rush home.'

This met with a peeved humph.

With the kettle humming away beside him, MJ rested his back against the kitchen bench, crossed his arms over his broad chest, and fixed her with a level gaze. 'Don't tell me things didn't pan out for you up there either?'

'Alright, I won't tell you.'

'So...?'

'It was ... awful, MJ.' She dragged a hand over her face and slumped into the nearest chair. 'Simply ... awful. You can't know how much I regret making that damn trip.' Her voice broke, and tears welled in her eyes. 'Talk about a total disaster.' With a loud sniff, she turned her face away to swipe at the tears.

'So, you found out ... about Cal.' At the sink, MJ felt hope rising. Hope followed by guilt. It was wrong to feel glad about what must've been a terrible experience for her.

Thinking he meant Cal's cavalier attitude, she muttered, 'Oh yeah, I found out alright.' Then, struck by something in his voice, she flicked MJ a perturbed glance.

He didn't notice, was distracted by his own turbulent emotions. 'Those mining camps,' he said in as soothing a tone as he could manage, 'are notorious for that sort of thing, Lib.'

When she merely frowned at him, he charged on. 'Blokes away from home for long stretches of time can get real ... lonely ... 'n do things they wouldn't normally consider doing.' She still didn't speak, and when he noticed the colour draining from her face, he went on hastily.

'Some justify havin' casual hook-ups by sayin' "A man's not a camel", but what it boils down to is—'

With a strangled cry Libby leapt to her feet. 'What the *hell* are you suggesting, MJ?'

He froze and gaped at her for long, fraught seconds, the kettle coming loudly to the boil in the silence.

'Are you trying to say that Cal,' and she gulped, 'is cheating on me? Is *that* what you're saying, MJ?'

'Lib, I—' He stopped when she threw up a hand.

'No need to answer. I can see from your face that's *exactly* what you're saying.'

'But I thought you—'

'I what?'

'I thought you knew. You said ... you regretted going on the trip, that it was a ... total disaster.'

'And it was, but not for the reason *you* think. And by the way, whatever gave you the idea Cal was....' The words caught in her throat, snagging on her own recently acquired suspicions and angering her further.

MJ's expression grew more pained as he said through tight lips, 'There's been some ... talk ... around town.'

'Oh, people are talking about me?' Her mouth twisted. 'Why am I not surprised.' She thrust both hands on her hips. 'But I *am* surprised at you, MJ, for buying in to idle gossip. I thought you were better than that.'

'It wasn't just idle gossip, Lib—'

'Really? Pray tell, what was it then?'

He gave a hard blink. 'You know old Mick Rawlins?' At

her curt nod, he went on. 'Apparently his granddaughter's boyfriend works up there too, at the mine.'

'And he's the one spreading rumours about Cal?'

MJ said nothing, merely stared despondently at her.

'And you didn't suspect he might simply be, oh I don't know, making trouble for Cal?'

She couldn't know that MJ was asking himself the same question, and wondering why he'd been so quick to assume the worst about Callum McDougall. The bloke had done nothing to deserve such eager condemnation. Nothing, that is, except....

'No answer for that, MJ? Well then, tell me this. Why, if he's playing the field, would Cal be showering me with gifts like that beautiful palomino mare, and *this* gorgeous bling,' and she thrust up her arm to shake the sparkling bracelet in his face.

'But he didn't....' MJ's voice trailed off.

'Didn't what? Meet my father's impossible expectations of any boyfriend of mine?' Charging into the kitchen she fronted up to him, eyes flashing. 'And of course you'd share Dad's expectations, taking his side like you always do.'

MJ stared at her, his face working. She was upset, and had every right to be. Why add disenchantment to the list of things she was dealing with right now?

'Lib, I—'

As if he hadn't spoken, she rose on tiptoes to put her face close to his and prodded him in the shoulder with a cruel finger. 'Come on, then. Be a man and tell me.'

When she prodded him again, his fist flew up and he grabbed her hand. His eyes were dark, angry slits.

She tossed back her head and laughed wildly. 'Or maybe Cal didn't meet your "suitable neighbour" criteria, hmm?' She leaned in closer, wrenching at her imprisoned fist, unhinged with anguish and rage. 'I'd like to know, MJ. What *exactly* didn't Cal do? Go on, I'm listening.' She looked up, flushed and challenging, eyes fixed on his face.

The intensity of his expression was something she'd never seen on him before. In sudden panic she pulled back, but he closed his arms around her and hauled her against his hard-muscled chest.

And in that moment, that breathless, pulsing moment before his head lowered and his mouth claimed hers, she could see nothing but the fire burning behind his dark eyes.

18

The kettle finished boiling and switched off, leaving a wintry silence in the room. Outside, the magpie had stopped singing and the cattle were quiet for a change. It was as if the whole farm, the whole world perhaps, was holding its breath.

Libby remained motionless, aghast, the fingers of one hand trembling against her mouth. MJ hadn't moved either, stood staring into her face while a slew of emotions crossed his own.

'Lib....' His voice was hoarse. He made to touch her face and the movement jolted her into action.

Shoving his hand aside, she stepped back from his arms. Still she didn't speak, could find no words for the emotions running riot within.

Anger, shock, indignation.

And her totally unexpected, *adulterous,* response.

This wasn't Cal, the man she loved. This was MJ, her helpful neighbour, fellow grazier, lifelong friend. There were no grounds for him to do what he just did, and *certainly* no grounds for her to respond the way she had. So then ... why?

Why?

Searching her feelings only revealed all-out turmoil.

It just happened, that's all.

Her face flamed as alarm joined the riot of emotions.

Cal mustn't ever get wind of this!

Guilt joined the fray.

So now I'm keeping secrets from the man in my life?

Consternation followed.

At a time when our relationship could use some reinforcement.

Blame hit the ground running.

Damn you, MJ! What have you done?

Drawing a rasping breath, she croaked the first words her reeling brain could come up with. 'Get out.'

'What?' He stiffened, frowning.

She swallowed and said again, more firmly this time, 'Get out.'

'Look, Lib, let me—'

Dragging a hand across her mouth as if to wipe away the kiss and her shameful—*traitorous*—surrender to it, she ground out, 'Didn't you hear what I said?'

'No, wait. Lib.' He squeezed his temples with urgent, unsteady fingers. 'I'm sorry— '

She threw up a hand. 'Don't speak to me.'

'But—'

'Just go,' and she pointed to the door. 'Leave. *Now.*' Her voice cracked. 'And ... and ... stay away from me. I don't want to s-see you again.'

At her words his body went rigid and he stared back at her, his eyes wide, devastated. 'You don't mean that Lib. Look, I've said I'm sorry. You just need—'

'DON'T you DARE try to t-tell me what I need. You don't KNOW what I need.' Now the tears were streaming down her face, her lips quivering, whole body shuddering from the force of her inner upheaval. 'But I'll tell you one th-thing I n-need.' Whirling around to plough through the debris, she wrenched the front door fully open, uncaring when it ground over broken glass on the floor. 'I need you OFF my property. NOW! And don't c-come back, *ever.*'

He opened his mouth only to close it again as he slowly, robotically, navigated his way to where she stood, stony-faced, holding the door open. When he stepped outside onto the veranda and turned as if to say something more, she used all her strength to swing the door closed in his shocked face.

The image of which came back to haunt her for the rest of the day and all that night.

. . .

In the following days she did her best to force the memory of that kiss to the back of her mind. Between the house and the hayshed she had plenty to keep herself busy, but even that didn't stop her treacherous thoughts from returning to the shameful scene with MJ.

And replaying it over and over in her mind's eye, especially at night when her defences were down.

Having stood outside her door a while, hoping she might reconsider, MJ had finally given up when he heard her launch into a noisy clean-up as if sending him a signal.

That she was unlikely *ever* to forgive him for the stupid thing he'd done.

Still, as he set off on the short trip home, he kept glancing back at the *Boronia* homestead in case she'd rushed out, thinking better of throwing him off the property.

It didn't happen.

And he couldn't expect her to forgive him.

What had got into him, kissing her like that? He *knew* her heart belonged to Cal, her loyalty to the slimy lowlife made that fact all too plain.

Hadn't he even decided, perhaps a tad optimistically, that he'd come to terms with the situation? So why blow things now and jeopardise their long-term friendship, their neighbourly partnership?

He drove home swearing loudly, punching the unfortunate steering wheel with the heel of one hand while admonishing himself for being a damnable, mindless, self-sabotaging idiot.

Agonising over the scene later, he concluded her proximity had been his undoing. Even when they worked together he took care to ensure they didn't get physically close. Having her up against him like that, hot with anger, her breasts heaving, the scent of her filling his nostrils, all led to his loss of self-control. Control he'd initiated years ago and maintained over the years.

Until now.

And to be honest, he couldn't deny the part hope played in this little fiasco. The hope that the 'disastrous' visit with Cal might lead to an opportunity for him, MJ, to step into the breach. The hope that finally, after denying his feelings for so long, he might have a chance to tell her something important.

That he loved her. Always had, always would.

And yes, he should've declared his feelings well before this, but had never found the right time. He'd gather his courage only to hear she'd started up with some other bloke, and by the time she was free again, *he'd* be seeing someone.

Past history. Right now he was unattached, and Libby....

At the memory of her soft, womanly scent, he felt again her warm lips and body against his, and recalled her breath-taking, if short-lived, response to his kiss. The sensual memories aroused ardent stirrings, but they were swamped in the very next instant by self-reproach.

This is what comes of those types of thoughts. Now I have to keep my distance, at least until she cools off.

And I can only hope she does.

Back from inspecting the soul-crushing remains of her hayshed that evening, Libby trudged inside just as, from somewhere beneath the debris, the phone gave one final ring before voicemail took the call.

She clicked her tongue. There were calls to make, and she needed to check her messages. One of her first calls would be to the insurance company to lodge claims both for the storm damage to the shed, and malicious damage to the house and contents.

Standing wearily in the kitchen doorway, she tried not to feel overwhelmed by the remaining mess. While she'd managed to clear paths by sweeping the debris into piles, she would need to sort through those piles when she had a chance.

Heaving a sigh, she moved to crouch beside where she thought the ring might've come from. After digging through dented cans of food, popped bags of salted nuts and potato chips—Cal's favourite snacks—shards of smashed crockery, and broken jam and honey jars whose sticky and flour-sprinkled contents oozed unhelpfully over her hands, she found the phone.

With a quick wipe of her sticky hands down the legs of her pants, Libby carefully extracted the handset and its cord. Rising, she returned the phone to its spot on the kitchen bench, which, like the cooking area of sink, stove, and fridge, was now cleared of wreckage, creating a kind of oasis amid the mess.

Keeping her back to the remaining chaos, she dialled voicemail and listened to the messages. There were a few, including one from her parents asking her to call, and another from a girlfriend inviting her to a glassware party.

Glassware?

She eyed the shard-strewn piles nearby and gave a grim smile.

I might even go to that party.

The next message was from MJ—how dare he!—saying only that he was sorry—well *duh!*—followed by one from someone calling herself Prue. A telemarketer no doubt.

Stabbing a vengeful finger on the DELETE button for those last two messages, and making a mental note to return the other calls and phone the insurance company when she felt stronger, Libby hung up and turned back to the mess.

It wasn't going to clean itself, and there was nobody else to lend a hand. Cal wasn't here to help, and she didn't even have MJ to call on now.

He was lost to her.

Maybe both men were.

An intense longing rose to engulf her and she doubled over as if in physical pain.

A familiar pain.

The pain of abject loneliness.

This was a loneliness more devastating and intense than she'd ever experienced before, shadowed by something darker and more ominous.

A gathering of menacing storm clouds at the edges of her psyche.

19

Libby jerked awake and rolled onto her back with a groan. That damned early caller deserved to be answered by voicemail.

Then she glanced at the bedside clock.

Not so early after all.

How much sleep had she managed to catch during the night?

Not much.

Right when she needed rest—needed to shrug off the heavy heart and demotivating fatigue, needed all her strength and wits about her—instead she'd lain sleepless hour after frustrating hour. And now, mere minutes it seemed after finally dropping off, she'd been woken by a phone call.

Better not be MJ ringing again. What part of GET LOST did he not understand?

Then again, it might be Cal, returning her call from late last night.

Dragging herself out of bed, she plodded bleary-eyed to the kitchen and dialled the number for voicemail. There were two messages. The first was from her mother.

'We got your message love, saying you were heading back home, but you didn't say why.'

A prudent move, judging by the concern in Rhonda's voice.

Imagine if I'd blurted out the whole story.

'Hope you're alright?' the message continued. 'Please call as soon as you get a chance. Just want to make sure everything's okay.'

Libby dragged a hand over her face. She couldn't put off responding for too long, but wished she had more time to gather her strength.

Much as I don't want to give them more bad news, they need to know what's happened, on the farm at least. And if they ask after Cal, and my fiasco of a trip....

Her stomach clenched.

Can't face that yet. I'll just ... keep their attention focused on the farm.

'None of the hay was salvageable? None at all?'

In contrast to her father's stout, matter-of-fact tone over the phone line, Libby's was wearily stoic. 'What wasn't burnt was water damaged.'

After a peeved grunt, Dave barked, 'And you've arranged for a replacement load of hay?'

'Yes, Murray has delivered it already. And before you ask, I've covered the bales in tarps, in case of more wet weather.'

'Good. Did you order enough to see you through 'til the shed's been repaired?'

A pensive crease formed in Libby's brow. 'I think so.'

'When did the builder say he could start work on the repairs?'

'Not 'til next month. He has to order in timber and other supplies.'

Another grunt, of resigned acknowledgement this time. 'You've contacted the insurance company about both the shed and the break-in at the house?'

'Yes, Dad.'

'And the Police have been alerted about the break-in?'

It was like her father was ticking items off a checklist.

'Yes, Dad. I told you, MJ called them straight after it happened.' It stung having to say his name. She was still smarting from his kiss, the intimate moment between them which left her feeling ... strange ... whenever she recalled it.

Exactly what that feeling meant was something she continued to shy away from.

Her long-suffering tone must've got to Dave, for he snapped, 'Look Lib, I just want to make sure everything's been taken care of.'

'And that you're coping okay,' Rhonda called more gently from in the background. Then she said, 'Dave, put the phone on speaker so I can talk too.'

Libby heard rustling sounds, and then her mother's voice came over clearly. 'I hate to think of you dealing with all this alone, love. If only Cal was home—'

'Yes, but he isn't.' Libby tried to disguise the sharpness of her words with a fake cough. Her mother was so attuned to things like that.

'Maybe we should come down there,' Dave muttered as if talking to himself.

'Yes, we could help with the clean-up,' Rhonda added, 'and give you some support. You've had such a rough trot, even having to rush home from visiting Cal. He must've been so worried—'

'You don't need to drop everything and rush here,' Libby cut in. The last thing she wanted was her hyper-observant mother and interfering, if well-meaning, father watching her every move. And Rhonda would view each tiny alteration in her daughter's body language—and lately some of those were probably more acute than tiny—as meaningful, which would lead to questions Libby wasn't prepared to answer.

Was a long way short of being ready to answer.

Becoming an expressionless automaton wouldn't work either. After trying that approach before, she knew it only led to more questions.

'Thanks for the offer, but I'm on top of things, truly.' At her father's unconvinced silence, Libby added hastily, 'And if anything changes, I promise to let you know ASAP.'

'Well, I do have a specialist appointment this week, one I've had to wait a whole month for, so I don't really want to reschedule....' The frown was obvious in Rhonda's voice. 'But are you sure you can cope for the moment?'

'I'm sure, Mum. And speaking of coping, there are other messages on my voicemail that could be important, so I'd better go.'

'Alright,' her father said gruffly. 'But let us know once you hear from the insurance company. Or the Police. Or the builder—'

'Don't worry, Dad,' Libby said with indulgent forbearance, 'I'll keep you posted.'

'Right-oh.'

After they chimed, 'Bye, love,' and she ended the call, Libby sagged against the wall, closed her eyes, and let her head fall back against the panelling.

This is all so exhausting....

She stayed there, simply breathing in and out, trying to clear her mind of negative thoughts. After a minute or two she remembered the second message. Pushing herself off the wall, she returned to the phone.

This message was from the same woman as before, the one calling herself Prue. With an irate click of her tongue, Libby was about to delete the message when she heard the woman say she was calling from the Seedy Creek mining camp.

Seedy Creek. Where Cal worked.

Was she a co-worker?

Had something happened to him?

Oh no, no....

The blood drained from her face.

Is that why she rang yesterday, to tell me he'd had an accident? And I deleted her message!

With urgent, unsteady fingers, she hastily pressed the number to return the call.

'Hello?'

'Is that....' When the words came out like squeaks, Libby cleared her throat and tried again. 'Prue?'

'That's me. Who's this?'

'My name's Libby Barnes. You ... left a message for me?'

'Libby B—' A pause, and then, 'Oh yeah, little Suzy Homemaker,' said with distaste and a hint of triumph. 'I have a message for you alright. It's to do with the bastard you call a boyfriend.'

'What are you talking about?'

'Cal McDougall. He's your bloke, isn't he?'

'Well ... yes. But what about him? I don't underst—'

'Oh you will, when you hear what the two-timing slime-ball's been gettin' up to.'

. . .

Moments—which to her felt like eons—later, Libby managed to hang up in the ranting woman's ear. Then the receiver slipped from her nerveless fingers to clatter first to the bench and then to the floor as she remained rooted to the spot, snatches of the woman's harsh words ringing in her ears.

'... led me on, made me think we had something ... even stripped at a bucks night 'cos the bastard asked me to ... went to his unit afterwards ... found him shacked up with that trollop of a pay mistress ... only using me, the no-good, two-timing ... deserves to be kicked to the kerb....' And the final thrust, 'Of course *Mr Perfectly Fine*,' said with an audible sneer, 'is no doubt using you too.'

Now the words of Taylor Swift's hit song rang in Libby's ears.

How could you, Cal?

A sob escaped but she bit back the next and put a hand to her chest.

Wait! Do I blindly accept the words of some stranger phoning me out of the blue? What if this Prue is just troublemaking like those two creeps in the mining camp?

'Another of the Tom Cat's conquests, are ya?' they'd taunted. And, 'We're Casanova's ... er ... Cal's mates.'

She could brush them off as troublemakers, but Cal's recent behaviour was harder to ignore. Greeting her like a pariah and not letting her in ... because he wasn't dressed and his place was a mess? Since when did he care about things like that? It didn't ring true.

And now this Prue person and her allegations.

The blood in Libby's veins turned from ice to lava.

Did Cal send her away because the 'trollop of a pay mistress' was inside his donga ... in his bed perhaps?

Head swimming, she slumped into a nearby chair.

No, no, no....

MJ had said there'd been gossip around town. Was it sympathy for the 'scorned woman' she saw in the faces at the post office, stockfeed merchant, and grocery store? Talk was cheap, but in light of the other evidence....

Putting her head between her knees, she told herself to keep breathing.

MJ was right....

His words replayed in her frazzled mind.

'Blokes away from home for long stretches of time can get real ... lonely ... 'n do things they wouldn't normally.'

He was right, and I threw him out.

Another sob escaped her.

Even told him to stay away, that I didn't want to see him again.

As the scene continued replaying in her mind, she stiffened and lifted her chin.

Wait just a minute. After first trying to justify Cal's actions, MJ then went and kissed me?

What the hell was that about? What's happening to me and the people around me?

Am I going crazy?

At a continual, insistent buzz from the phone receiver she bent to retrieve it. An instant after she dropped it in the phone cradle it rang, making her jump. Without thinking she snatched it up again and put it to her ear.

'Lib? Is that you, love?'

Squeezing her eyes shut and cursing herself for taking the call, she managed to croak, 'Yeah, Mum.'

'Oh, good. Look, I was thinking about the last time we spoke. You didn't sound very happy when talking about Cal, so I was wondering ... is everything alright between you two?'

Libby's throat constricted.

So much for keeping their focus on the farm....

She swallowed.

How should she answer?

A simple, 'No, Mum, everything isn't alright,' would only prompt more intense questioning, to which she'd answer ... what? How about, 'It turns out that while I've been busy missing Cal like a gullible, trusting fool, he's been busy two-timing ... maybe three-timing ... me. And I'm apparently the last person in the district to hear about it.' Oh yeah, that'd go down *really* well with her parents.

And it wasn't enough she had to confront the agonising truth, that despite his promises Cal was moving on, leaving her alone once more. No, that was only *one* bad news item in her growing list of blunders.

If she were to blurt out everything, it would end up

being something like, 'On top of that, I've burned my bridges with MJ, who's only ever done right by me and even tried to do the same by Cal. And while the lightning strike on the hayshed wasn't my doing, I was away at the time— chasing after Cal, how pathetic—which allowed the fire to get a hold on the stored hay.

'And did I mention the badly burned arm MJ copped while fighting the blaze? My fault. So was the break-in, which appears to be payback for dobbing in the gang suspected of injuring Harry. Add to everything else the loss of Dad's hard-won lease thanks to my high-handedness, and you'll come to realise, as I have, that the bad stuff happening lately has all been my fault.'

My fault.

All *my fault.*

The naysayers were right, she was useless at everything and should never have taken over the farm.

As her thoughts spiralled downward, the menacing clouds on the edges of her consciousness grew blacker and denser, and closed in.

'Lib?' her mother urged. 'You still there, love?'

She opened her mouth.

Couldn't bear to say the words.

Closed her mouth again.

Gripped the receiver more tightly.

Squeezed her eyes shut and took a breath.

Opened her mouth.

The words lodged in her throat, would come no further.

Closed her mouth again.

Loosened her grip on the receiver.

Slowly lowered her hand until it hovered above the cradle.

'You there, L—'

Click.

20

As he sauntered into the wet mess Rod spied Cal hunched over the bar, the beer glass in front of him caked in dried froth. With only a handful of customers to serve, barmaid Prue wasn't run off her feet, but when Cal raised the glass to indicate he wanted a refill, she ignored him.

Grinning smugly, Rod strode to the bar and plonked his skinny butt on a stool, swivelling to stare at Cal. When that garnered no response, he nudged him on the shoulder. 'G'day, mate.'

Flicking him a glance Cal said coldly, 'What do *you* want?'

'Can't a bloke have a drink with a mate without gettin' interrogated? 'N speakin' of drinks, this is somethin' of a dry argument, isn't it?' Rod flicked Cal's beer glass with a finger. 'And a long drought, by the looks of things.' He gazed around. 'Not that busy in here. A bloke should be able to get his glass refilled faster'n that, 'specially with the lovely Prue on the job.'

When Rod flicked the glass again, Cal snatched it up.

'My oh my.' Sitting back, Rod eyed him gleefully. 'Done something wrong by our Prue, have ya?' He shook his head. 'Thought a lover boy like you would know better than that. What's the saying about a "woman scorned"—'

'Shut the hell up.' Banging his glass on the bar, Cal swivelled to face him. 'I just want to sit here and have a quiet drink, so why don't you bugger off and find someone else to pester.'

'Now, now,' Rod crooned. 'Don't take it out on me if you're havin' woman troubles.' His eyes glinted. 'Or should I say *women* troubles?'

Cal gave a puzzled frown as Prue, still ignoring him, moved up the bar to serve Rod.

When she asked, 'The usual?' Rod flashed her a wink. 'Thanks, darlin'.' He watched her put a fresh glass under the chilled beer tap and begin dispensing the frothy amber liquid. 'The lovely Prue here deserves to be treated like a princess,' he said with an oily smile. 'Don'cha, darlin'?'

She kept her head bent over the filling glass.

'So if y'ask me, anyone who doesn't treat her proper, deserves everythin' he gets.' Rod turned back to eye Cal. 'Same for those that don't treat their *friends* proper.'

The crease in Cal's forehead deepened. 'What are you jabbering about?'

'Well, look at how you treated me 'n Snake the other day.' Putting a hand to his heart, Rod faked a wounded expression. 'Our feelings were hurt.' He batted his eyelids at Cal. 'Poor Snake may never recover.'

Swearing loudly, Cal made a grab for Rod's neck, only to withdraw his hand when he noticed the publican emerge from the back office.

'That's right,' Rod said blithely, 'you don't wanna get banned from the place. It'd mean an awful long time between drinks.' He sniggered. 'Best you stay all sweetness 'n light, mate.' When Prue put a dewy, froth-topped glass on the bar in front of him, he handed her some notes and said grandly, 'Keep the change, love.' Turning back to the scowling Cal, he smirked. 'See? *That's* how mates should treat each other, not like what you did the other day.'

'You're no mates of mine,' Cal snarled, 'you and that weirdo you hang around with.'

'See? This is what I'm talkin' about. Callin' us names and so forth. And why? All me 'n Snake were doin' was keepin' your little woman company while she was waitin' for you to finish....' He ran his tongue slowly over his lips. '...whatever it was you were doin'.'

Slapping an open palm on the bar, Cal growled, 'Get lost, Rod, or get carried out. Your choice.'

'Oh, so that's how it is.' After taking a noisy slurp of beer, Rod wiped the back of a hand across his dripping mouth and rose nonchalantly to his feet. Bending, he murmured in Cal's ear, 'Spoken to your little woman at home recently?'

Jerking his head away, Cal narrowed his eyes at the other man. 'What are you getting at?'

Rod straightened to grin down at him. 'Oh, just tryin' to help a mate. Then again, I'm sure you're already aware how fast news travels.' He indicated the pinch-faced Prue behind the bar. 'Of course bad news travels faster than most, and not just within the camp. So if I were you, *mate,*' and he gave a snide wink, 'I'd be checkin' how things are at home.'

The more her parents phoned, the less she could face telling them all that had happened.

They left messages on the landline and even on her mobile, despite knowing only too well how unreliable mobile reception was in the area. The first two messages were from her mother, extending loving but increasingly concerned appeals for her to call back.

Then her father left a similar request, followed by a more forceful demand, before finally opting for tough love. 'If you don't ring back soon, you can expect us, or perhaps the local constabulary, to turn up on the doorstep.'

From where she sat at the kitchen table, forehead

resting on her crossed arms, Libby groaned and lifted her chin.

Now he's threatening to send the Police around?

It's all too much!

Sagging back against the chair, she swept a gaze around the living area where piles of debris still waited to be sorted through.

Way too much.

Her throat constricted.

I can't face it ... any of it.

Overcome by the urge to move, she sprang to her feet.

I have to get away from this ... from them ... from everything.

About to head down the corridor to her room, she stopped.

What's the point in packing a bag? Where can I get away to?

She couldn't afford expensive accommodation, and *certainly* wasn't running to Cal. And if she went to her parents' place for a break she'd have to open up about everything, and suffer her mother's sympathy and her father's 'told you so', the latter being infuriating whether spoken or not. Anyway, they had enough to deal with without having more of her troubles dumped on them.

And with MJ's kiss hanging between them, she couldn't even avail herself of his sympathetic ear.

So where could she find even a smidgen of comfort?

Throwing her hands in the air with an anguished, 'Oh!' she made for the liquor cabinet.

Desperate times...

Flinging open the door, she stared at the cabinet's contents, and her spirits plummeted further.

Of the few bottles remaining from her father's collection, all were empty bar one. And that one bottle contained mere dregs of Irish whisky.

Damn you, Cal. How could you help yourself to stuff and not bother replacing it?

The answer came in a replay of that Prue woman's bitter words. '... Mr Perfectly Fine ... no doubt using you too.'

Muttering, 'Shut up, shut up, shut up,' under her breath, Libby grabbed the bottle, unscrewed the lid, and downed the fiery contents. In the midst of the coughing fit that followed came a hint of comforting warmth.

More.

I need more.

She dropped to her haunches to conduct a thorough search of the cabinet.

Only empty bottles.

And then she remembered something Cal had done after coming home from a 'really bad' day at work.

Leaving the cabinet door hanging open and the empty whisky bottle on the floor, she rose to make for the bedroom, the room she'd shared with Cal but would no longer. Sobs caught in her throat as she went to his side— what *had* been his side—of the bed, to yank open the drawer in the bedside table.

And found what she was looking for.

~

Should he leave things as they are, let the situation play out?

If that mongrel Rod was right and Libby *had* heard what was going on up here, it would probably spell the end of their relationship. Was that such a bad thing? Lib had proved to be more needy than he'd expected, and what he had with Alinta was proving better than he could've imagined. Although ... the other night she'd made a troubling comment about leaving her husband.

Cal's self-satisfied grin faded.

If it wasn't just pillow talk, would she expect some sort of long-term commitment from him? He wasn't up for any serious obligation, and Alinta struck him as the type to want all the bells and whistles. She might even anticipate another big, flashy wedding.

Marriage?

He winced.

Being tied to one woman for life?

Not something he would ever commit to. But if things panned out the way he feared, his refusal to commit could become a sticking point between him and Alinta.

So, where did all this leave him, assuming he and Libby did split?

Well, if he couldn't keep the fling with Alinta on the free 'n easy basis things might get a little dicey for him at the mine. There was always Prue to fall back on in camp—

though she was upset with him now, it wouldn't take much to bring her around—but if his contract with the mine wasn't extended or renewed ... what then?

He frowned.

If things did go pear-shaped it might be prudent to have the farm and Libby as a fall-back, so why burn his bridges when he might need them again?

Right. On his next days off he'd head to the farm and gauge how the land lay. Assuming she'd heard the gossip he could always smooth things over with Lib, she loved him enough to forgive him anything. And if her feathers were seriously ruffled, presenting her with a gift might help. Look at how thrilled she was when he gave her that damn horse. Women love bling, so this time he'd see about picking up a pretty trinket on the way there. Nothing too expensive, and not a ring of course. A necklace or pair of sparkly earrings should do it.

He gave a satisfied nod.

Luckily for him, women like Libby, Alinta, and even tough-nut barmaid Prue, were easy to manipulate ... if you went about it the right way. And wrapping women around his finger was something Callum McDougall did exceptionally well.

As she slid down the bedroom wall to the floor, her outstretched hands unable to prevent the fall, the garnets on her wrist caught and scraped against the painted surface. The sound registered through the miasma filling her mind, and with a guttural cry she clawed at the once cherished and now detested bracelet. After managing to wrench it off, she hurled it away with a strangled sob.

The movement sent her toppling face-first to the floor. From there she crawled into the corner, feeling the way as her eyes rolled in her swimming head. Collapsing against the wall, she huddled there, desperate to cloak herself with its detached anonymity.

Moments later, as she crumpled senseless to the carpet, the empty hip flask rolled out of her hand and came to rest near the discarded garnet bracelet. The label bore the handwritten words, *First Batch,* and a date.

In Callum McDougall's familiar scrawl.

21

'Gidday, MJ. Dave Barnes 'ere.'

'Hey, Dave. How's things?'

'Look mate, sorry to be a bother but I've got a favour t'ask.'

'Ask away.'

'Rhonda and I are worried about our girl. Been tryin' to get 'er on the phone all day, but keep gettin' her damn voicemail. And she's not returnin' our calls for some reason.'

At the worry and frustration in Dave's voice, cold droplets of fear splattered on MJ's heart.

'This is why we hate living so *damn* far away,' Dave rasped, ''specially when it wasn't our choice to leave in the first place....' He sighed, impatient with himself. 'Anyway, Lib's had something of a tough time lately MJ, so—'

'No worries, Dave. I'll go over and check everything's okay.'

'Can't tell ya how much we appreciate it, mate. Get 'er to give us a call, will ya?'

On the drive to *Boronia Station* MJ tried not to think about Libby's last words to him, 'I don't want to see you again.' Surely she didn't mean that? Although ... he *had* done the wrong thing by kissing her.

Squirming in the seat, he firmed his grip on the steering wheel and pushed those thoughts aside.

Dave and Rhonda are relying on me to check on her, so that's what I'm gonna do ... that's ALL I'm gonna do.

When his knock at her front door went unanswered, he glanced over at the shed. Her battered ute and tractor were both parked there, so she hadn't gone out or ventured far from the homestead.

Must be around the place somewhere.

He made his way to the back door, knowing he'd find it open—nobody in the bush bothered too much about security. After kicking off his boots he stood in the doorway and called, 'Hello?'

The only response was an accusing, eerie silence.

'You there, Lib?'

Nothing.

Frowning, he stepped inside. The house felt ... different. Kind of ... devoid of life.

Apprehension crawled beneath his skin.

Where was she?

As he took in the piles of debris still awaiting attention, the dirty crockery at the sink, the blowflies buzzing around the rubbish bin, dread clawed at his insides.

No way would she leave the place in this condition if she were going away for any length of time. And her parents would know of any planned trip, nothing surer. They were a close family, one he'd always wished he could join for real.

Feeling like an intruder, he made his way along the corridor in socked feet, checking each room as he passed. When he reached the doorway to her bedroom, he swept a glance over the unmade bed and the bundle of dirty clothes in one corner.

Not here either.

About to move on, something made him stop and turn back. Stepping into the room, he peered at the crumpled bundle on the floor.

Not dirty clothes at all.

It was a body, coiled wretchedly on the floor.

Libby!

Muttering, 'Oh no, no,' he darted across the room to kneel beside her, gently shaking her and saying her name over and over.

No flicker of response, and her skin was cold and clammy to the touch.

Bending over her, he felt for a pulse. When his shaking fingers located faint thumps and she gave a tiny moan, he bowed his head and let out a huge breath before sagging to the floor, his back against the wall.

Digging out his mobile he went to phone triple zero for Emergency Services, only to curse when the screen showed no available signal.

Damn the district's bad reception! He'd have to use the landline. About to get up, he glimpsed something red on the floor.

Her bracelet, lying beside a metal ... hip flask?

Hastily scooping them up, he slipped the bracelet into a pocket but kept hold of the flask.

What was it doing here?

Frowning, he gave it a shake.

Empty.

Lifting it to his nose, he sniffed and pulled a face. Judging by the harsh smell, the flask had contained some pretty rough stuff. Home-brewed spirit maybe? Still frowning, he turned to her again, touched gentle fingers to her lips, and then lifted his fingers to his nose.

Liquor of some kind, no doubt about it.

Had the flask been full when she brought it in here? If so, she must've drunk it dry.

He ran a measuring glance over it. Full, it would hold around ... ten?... shots, or about a cupful of spirit.

After gazing intently into her pale, unresponsive face, and listening to her shallow breathing, he gave her another gentle shake and called her name.

She wasn't just drunk, not if he was any judge.

Then he noticed the handwritten label on the flask.

At some stage it had contained home-brewed spirits.

Dave was a beer drinker and not the type to carry a hip flask, so it must be Cal's.

Where would he have got home-brewed liquor?

More importantly, was the stuff safe for a non-drinker like Lib to consume?

Oh no. What if...?

Leaping to his feet MJ raced to the kitchen, where he snatched the telephone receiver from its cradle and dialled triple zero. Once satisfied an ambulance was on its way, he hurried back to Libby's side. Lifting her limp body into his arms he sat cradling her against his chest, stroking her hair and murmuring words of comfort until the paramedics arrived.

He watched anxiously while they assessed her, then followed as they stretchered her into the ambulance. Before they left, he tapped one of the paramedics on the shoulder and handed him the flask with a meaningful glance. The man frowned at him and then at the flask, before giving a nod of understanding when he grasped the significance.

As he stood staring after the departing ambulance MJ knew what he had to do next, but was dreading phoning

Libby's parents. They'd be distressed enough by the news their daughter had been rushed unconscious to hospital. The fear that she could be the victim of deadly methanol poisoning he'd keep to himself, at least for now.

When hospital visiting hours came around the following afternoon, MJ was heading to Libby's room when he ran into her parents in the corridor. They were on their way out and appeared heart-wrenchingly glad to see him, but their drawn, white faces, and the way Rhonda clung to Dave like she hadn't the strength to stand on her own, left him dry-mouthed and speechless.

As though needing to share with another who knew and cared for their daughter, they poured out their desperate concerns about her state of mind.

Wrapping a hand around MJ's arm as if to absorb some of his strength, a clearly distraught Rhonda stared into his face. 'I don't understand,' she said tearfully, 'Lib's refusing to speak to anyone, even us. And she's not eating or drinking either.' She sniffed. 'Can't blame her though, hospital food and all.' Releasing his arm, she tried for a brave smile. 'So I'm going home to make some of her favourite dishes.'

Dave patted her hand and said gently, 'Go call the lift, love. I'll be there in a minute, just want a quick word with MJ.'

As the two men watched Rhonda trudge to the end of the corridor and press the button for the ancient, notoriously slow elevator, Dave said grimly, 'It was methanol poisoning.'

MJ's blood ran cold.

'The flask you found with her held traces of methanol contaminant. The doc believes that was the cause of her seizure and black-out.' Dave dragged a hand over his face. 'They had to pump out her stomach, but he reckons they caught it early enough to prevent long-term injuries.'

MJ released his held breath.

'And the fact she's alive is down to you, mate,' a watery-eyed Dave said, thumping him on the shoulder. 'How can we ever repay you?'

When MJ murmured, 'No repayment necessary,' Dave gave him another thump, before leaning in to say quietly, 'I've never seen that hip flask before. Have you?'

MJ shook his head.

'Must've been one of Cal's.' Dave glowered. 'Fancy that irresponsible bastard havin' contaminated spirits in the house in the first place, let alone leavin' 'em lyin' around for others to find. Ooh, how I'd like to get my hands on whoever made that filthy poison.'

His angry words jogged something in MJ's mind, but right now he needed to see Libby. Needed to assure himself she was indeed alive. When Dave excused himself and hurried to join Rhonda at the waiting lift, MJ made for Libby's room. He was pleased to find her awake, but at his approach she merely flicked him a dull glance and curled herself away to face the wall.

He paused, uncertain, before pulling a chair close to her bedside. Once seated he leaned his elbows on his knees, clasped his hands together, and said in his deep country drawl, 'Hey, Lib. How're you feelin'?'

No reply.

He touched tentative fingers to her arm. 'Saw your folks on their way out. They told me you're gonna be okay, after the docs pumped out your stomach.' He winced. 'Bet that wasn't pleasant.'

Her only response was to move even closer to the wall.

Sitting back in the chair he rubbed his healing arm and said slowly, 'It's great you're gonna be okay, but your Mum said you won't eat or drink anything.'

She continued staring at the wall.

'Hospital tucker may not be all that great, but surely you want that drip to come out?'

This finally got a reaction. When she rolled onto her back and lifted her hand to stare indignantly at the drip taped to it, he took the opportunity to fish something out of his shirt pocket. Noticing her eyes swivel his way, he leaned in and held up his hand. 'By the way, I thought you might want this.'

Blinking to see what he held between two strong, workmanlike fingers, she gave a start when he took her nearest hand in both his and pressed the jingling item into her palm. Closing her fingers over it he murmured, 'Did you know the garnet symbolises constancy in friendships?'

She frowned, recognising the words from the wrapping paper on Cal's surprise parcel. Then, as MJ released her hand, she opened it and gave a tiny gasp at what lay in her palm.

It was the first sound she'd made since he arrived, and he took it as a promising sign. That was until, with a rasping sob and an unsteady arm, she flung the bracelet weakly at the opposite wall.

22

With a baffled frown, MJ rose to retrieve the unfortunate bracelet from the polished linoleum floor. Returning to her bedside he held it up and asked, 'I thought you loved this?'

Once more turning her tear-streaked face to the wall, she curled away from him.

Folding the bracelet into his hand and rubbing the blood-red gems, MJ said gently, 'This isn't just a pretty trinket, Lib. The stones signify the constancy of our friendship, yours and mine.'

Constancy ... that word again.

She turned her head to stare blankly at him. 'Our friendship?' she whispered hoarsely. 'B-but ... why would Cal....'

Still eyeing the bracelet, MJ gave a tight-lipped smile. 'Yeah ... well that's the thing. *He* didn't. *I* did.'

'Y-you?' Her voice grew stronger. 'Wait, are you saying *you* gave me the bracelet?'

Had the beautiful, thoughtful gift she'd treasured so greatly not been from Cal at all?

Uncurling, she rolled onto her back to gaze at MJ in wonder. '*You* left the parcel on my doorstep?'

'Yep.'

'But ... why?'

He shrugged. 'Spotted the bracelet on a market stall and thought it'd suit you. An individual piece according to the stallholder, made from West Australian gems. I figured it was a bit special.'

Special?

Very.

And being a hand-crafted, individual piece of jewellery, no doubt expensive.

Raising his eyes, he smiled into hers. 'He also told me all about the properties of garnets. 'Course I forgot most of 'em,' and he flashed a lopsided grin, 'so looked 'em up online when I got home.'

Hence the computer-printed wrapping paper. She gave a faint nod.

'Anyway,' he went on, 'I figured the constancy element was more important than the others.'

While she, like a fool, had focused instead on the 'deepening of existing love'.

Swallowing a rising tide of contrition, she croaked, 'But it wasn't Christmas, or my birthday, or a gift-giving occasion of any kind. So why...?'

'I gave it to you because you're my friend,' he said gently, once more taking her hand in his, 'and going through a rough patch. I thought a surprise gift might lift your spirits.'

At the time he hadn't anticipated her assuming, perfectly naturally he realised now, that the gift was from Cal. In hindsight he should've written his name as sender on the parcel, but that would've spoiled the surprise. He'd planned to rock up and tell her personally and enjoy witnessing her reaction, only realising his mistake when it was too late.

Libby's eyes took on a faraway look as she lay absorbing the impact of his words, and running through events in her mind.

Was that why MJ had seemed out of sorts on the ride to Doc's, because she'd gone on and on about how Cal—'Mr Perfectly Fine' as that horrid woman called him—had gifted her the gorgeous bracelet? And all the while the true giver was riding tight-lipped beside her.

Why hadn't MJ said something to put her right?

Because he saw how happy I was and didn't want to burst my bubble.

Clearly, MJ cared more about her feelings than about being thanked for the gift. While Cal....

She scowled inwardly.

How could she have assumed such a meaningful, *perfect*, gift had come from him? He'd never cared enough to do the right thing by her, the farm, or her parents. Oh sure, he'd given her Rouge, but the mare had cost only time and a bit of extra fuel. And Libby suspected the gift was more a favour for the bloke wanting to re-home the horse than a show of love for her.

She gazed at the man sitting by her hospital bed, holding her chill hand in his large, warm one. He might've felt snubbed when Cal came on the scene, but MJ had been there for her in her time of need.

Was always there for her.

They'd both been born in this small country hospital, attended the district schools together, joined the local sporting and Rural Youth clubs, and grew up knowing everyone in the district.

MJ had laughed and danced with her at parties, weddings, bush dances and other shindigs, helped her choose winners at country racing carnivals, consoled her when fortune frowned, and commiserated with her when her teenage crushes bombed.

Then came the swirling waters of their adult years, when he proved to be a rock she could cling to, like the drowning magpie had clung to her rescue pole.

She'd risked losing all that for a shallow, no-good user like Callum McDougall?

I've been such a fool.

While she couldn't imagine life without MJ, she was

only now realising what he truly meant to her. Had he been waiting all this time for her to see him as the man he was, not just as her dependable neighbour and good mate?

Not just a fool, I've been a stupid BLIND fool.

A fat tear rolled down her cheek, but she smiled at him and raised her arm. Taking the hint, he refastened the bracelet and lifted her wrist to his lips, his eyes never leaving hers. In their warm darkness was something she'd glimpsed before, an intensity that was more than friendship. Only this time she recognised it for what it was.

'Thank you, MJ.' Remembering his kiss, she blushed and gave his hand a weak squeeze.

He squeezed back. 'You're welcome, Lib.'

They continued gazing at each other, and then she lifted impish eyebrows at him. 'Say ... what are the chances of you scoring me a sandwich from somewhere?'

His lips twitched. 'You hungry now?'

'And thirsty, so I've love a coffee too?'

'Not sure you should be eating just anything, but I'll go find out.' Setting down her hand, he gave it a pat and rose from the chair. Bending to drop a lingering kiss on her forehead he murmured, 'Back soon,' against her skin. 'Don't go anywhere.'

'I won't.' She held his hand until the last moment. 'And don't be long. I'm starving.'

. . .

After calling at the nurses' station and being informed that as it had been some hours since her procedure Libby was okay to eat solid food, and in fact hunger was a good sign, MJ stood at the coffee vending machine running his finger down the various options. In his other hand he held a bulging takeaway sandwich container.

About to press the button for a small—no, a medium—flat white, he heard someone approaching along the corridor behind him. Thinking it might be her parents returning, he glanced over a shoulder.

And although it wasn't either Dave or Rhonda Barnes, it *was* someone he knew.

Someone unwelcome, to say the least.

Callum *bloody* McDougall.

23

'Oy!' Stepping into the corridor, MJ threw up a hand. 'What the *hell* are you doin' here?'

Cal jerked to a stop and peered at him. 'Me? What are *you* doing here?'

'Visiting Libby.'

'Well then....' Cal's voice trailed off and he frowned. 'What's your name again?'

'MJ.' It was said with narrowed eyes.

'Well then, MJ, that makes two of us.'

'Why the hell would she want you to visit her, you two-timing bastard?'

At the challenge in MJ's words and body language, Cal stiffened and eyed him. While they were the same height this MJ character was more rugged, less good-looking of course, and right now appeared thoroughly riled.

Keeping an even, unconcerned tone Cal said, 'You're my partner's neighbour, right?'

At the partner reference, MJ bristled. 'You know who I am, so just answer the question.'

'I would,' Cal said smoothly, 'if it had anything to do with you, *neighbour*. But it doesn't, so I'll thank you to get out of my way.'

Moving closer, MJ growled in his face, 'You've got some nerve. It's thanks to *you* that Libby's here, in hospital.'

Appearing genuinely surprised, Cal barked, 'Thanks to me? How do you figure that?'

'She drank contaminated booze out of a flask that *you*,' and MJ poked an accusing finger into Cal's chest, just below the polo-player motif on his shirt, 'left lying around the house.'

'Contaminated booze?' Cal's face clouded and he took an abrupt step back. 'What are you talking about? Rhonda never said anything about that when she rang me last night, only that Libby had been taken to hospital. I assumed she'd had a farming accident.'

'They didn't know what had happened 'til after the medics carried out tests, which confirmed methanol poisoning.' MJ's tone lowered, became menacing. 'They tested your flask too, and confirmed it was the source of the poison.'

'Poison?' Cal blanched. 'Libby was *poisoned?*'

'That's right,' MJ snarled, 'and she could've died.'

'But ... she's not a spirit drinker.' As comprehension and

dismay registered on his face, Cal released a string of curses and dragged a shaking hand through his hair. 'I never thought....' Whirling around to thump the wall with the heel of a hand he growled, 'That first batch!'

First batch?

The words jogged something in MJ's brain, and he heard again Dave Barnes' voice in his head. '... like to get my hands on whoever made that filthy poison.' He'd said something similar after the recent bushfire too, about wanting to find whoever set the bush alight ... with an *illegal still*. MJ recalled thinking at the time he wouldn't like to be the responsible party. Dave Barnes could be formidable in certain situations, and especially where his daughter was concerned.

As the pieces slotted into place, MJ grabbed Cal by a shoulder and whirled him around. '*You* brewed that poison, didn't you.' It wasn't a question.

Cal merely stared at him from out of a pale, shocked face.

'And the bushfire they reckon was started by an illegal still, the one that destroyed old Reg Edwards' farm. *You* were behind that, weren't you?'

When MJ prodded him in the chest again, it roused Cal from his stunned daze. 'Illegal—' Pausing to clear his throat, he said more firmly, 'Illegal still? Bushfire? What are you goin' on about mate?' He gave a mocking smirk. 'Bit early in the day to be imbibing, isn't it?'

When MJ grabbed him by the shirt, Cal's expression

darkened. Tough or not, this cowpat needed to know he was punching above his weight. Snarling, 'Back off,' he shoved MJ in the chest. 'Lay another finger on me, *neighbour,* and you'll regret it.'

That did it.

Bunching, MJ clenched his fist and drew back his arm, preparing to deliver a powerful right to Cal's smug-looking jaw. Only an irate shout of, 'Hey! You two!' stopped him taking the swing.

The burly wardsman marched up to them, waving his arms. 'This is no place for grown men to be brawling,' he said sternly. 'If you wanna fight, do us all a favour and take it outside.'

Chagrined, MJ lowered his fist and muttered, 'Sorry, mate.'

Cal merely dropped his deflecting arm and tugged his shirt straight. 'The only place *I'm* going is to that room,' he snapped, pointing down the corridor. 'To visit MY girlfriend. ALONE.' He directed the last words at an incensed MJ.

The wardsman stared dubiously at them before moving on, saying, 'Fair enough. Just stay out of trouble, both of you.'

Ignoring the warning, Cal shot MJ a black look and snarled, 'And no pathetic hanger-on is gonna stop me,' before marching to Libby's room.

About to charge after him MJ paused, face working as

he choked back his anger. The wardsman was right, a hospital was no place for a punch-up. He stared thoughtfully down at his fist and slowly unclenched it.

There are other ways to skin a no-good cat.

His expression lifted a fraction. Taking out his mobile, he dialled a number, and while waiting for the call to be answered, tried not to agonise over what Libby's reaction would be to her latest visitor.

He hung up after a brief conversation, just as Dave Barnes appeared at his elbow.

'What'cha doin' out here, MJ?'

'Oh, just ... getting Lib a coffee, and somethin' to eat.'

Dave slapped him on the back. 'We *knew* you'd get her feelin' better. And don't worry about food, Rhonda sent me in with this,' and he held up a picnic basket from which lip-smacking aromas wafted. 'Plenty for you both.'

'Enough for three?' MJ asked grimly.

'I've already eaten.'

'I wasn't talkin' about you.'

Dave frowned at him. 'She's got another visitor?'

'Yeah.'

'Who?'

'Come on.' MJ set off along the corridor with Dave at his heels.

When they stopped outside the window to her room they saw Libby sitting up, staring open-mouthed at Cal, who was standing by her bed with his back to the window.

MJ's stomach lurched. She loved Cal so much ... would the bastard be able to smooth-talk his way out of this?

Beside him, Dave gave a growl and made a move for the doorway, until MJ's outstretched arm and quiet, 'Wait,' made him pause.

Focusing on Dave meant MJ missed seeing Cal bend to kiss Libby, who threw up a hand to stop him from getting close. Dave hadn't missed it, though. At his loud chuckle, MJ turned to see a frowning, less self-assured Cal dig in a pocket and hand something to Libby.

All three men watched as she first stared at the item and then held it up, dangling the necklace from two fingers so the pendant caught the overhead light. When her movements sent the garnet bracelet sliding up her arm, MJ couldn't help comparing the rich, timeless glow from the gems with the mass-produced pendant's gaudy and likely short-lived sparkle.

Then Cal said something and made as if to sit in the chair at her bedside, only to have Libby shake her head firmly at him.

Outside the window, Dave nudged MJ with an elbow and murmured, 'Reckon the mongrel's gettin' his marchin' orders.'

MJ said nothing, his entire focus on the drama playing out in the hospital room.

Cal appeared to be speaking and at one point reached for her hand, which Libby snatched away.

MJ's spirits continued to climb.

Cal spoke for a while longer, during which Libby's expression changed from angry and hurt to downright furious. Then she said something so loudly the watchers could almost hear it, and hurled the necklace at him.

Dave gave a whoop and said proudly, 'That's my girl. Knew she'd come to her senses eventually.'

MJ's spirits soared but he warned, 'It's not over yet.' And he wasn't just warning Dave.

Although Cal had stepped back to dodge the flying necklace, he held his ground and appeared to continue pleading his case to a stony-faced Libby. She barked something at him and pointed to the door. It took a few more barks and some forceful gesturing before he finally turned ... and saw a gleeful Dave and steely-eyed MJ staring in at him through the window.

Humiliation blazed in Cal's reddening face. Sticking out his chin, he marched from the room and would've bolted past the two men if MJ hadn't grabbed him by the arm.

Without looking at them, Cal ground out, 'Let go of me.'

'Why the hurry?' MJ asked mildly.

Cursing, Cal wrenched his arm free and turned to face him. 'None of your beeswax.'

MJ nudged Dave. 'Go see your daughter.'

'But—'

Shoving the packet of sandwiches at him, MJ said, 'Dave, go. I've got this.'

With some reluctance Dave complied.

Pushing his face close to MJ's, Cal spat, 'You've got *nothing.*'

'Oh, but I think I do.' As he spoke, MJ inclined his head toward the hospital room, where a concerned Libby was reaching for her father's hand while gazing out at the two warring men.

'Hah!' Cal sneered. 'Well, you're welcome to *that* little piece of—'

'Callum McDougall?' The commanding voice came from the corridor behind them.

Spinning around, Cal saw two uniformed police officers striding up to him. 'What the—'

'Callum McDougall,' one of the officers said, 'we'd like you to accompany us to the station.'

'Wait, what?' The blood drained from Cal's face. 'What's all this about?'

'We're investigating a case of methanol poisoning,' the officer said, coming to stand at his side. 'We'd also like to talk to you about a recent bushfire, and the operation of an illegal still.'

'You want to talk to me?' Cal tried for a winning smile but it came out like a wince. 'But ... I don't know anything.'

'Sir,' the officer said politely, 'we believe Don Weston is an associate of yours?'

Don.

What had the damned idiot done?

'He's already at the station, so if you'd accompany us there?'

'But I....' Cal's objection died in his throat. His shoulders slumped, and with a final guilty glance through the window at Libby, he gave a slow nod.

'This way, sir.'

Later that day, MJ sat on the edge of Libby's hospital bed holding her hand, while Dave stood behind Rhonda who was seated in the visitor's chair. All four were grinning over their takeaway coffee cups, and trying not to all talk at once.

Then Dave raised a hand and boomed, 'Got some more good news today.' When the others hushed, he said to Libby, 'Your mother and I were at the homestead, doin' a bit of cleaning up, when a Sergeant Wentworth of Brunswick Junction Police phoned. It seems someone tried to pawn Aunty Beth's clock, the one she gave you for your twenty-first birthday, Lib.'

'Oh?' Libby frowned. 'I love that clock, but ... hadn't realised they'd taken it.'

'Well,' Dave went on, clearly enjoying himself, 'they didn't take it far, only to Alan's pawn shop. Of course being a long time local, Al recognised the piece and knew about the break-in. So he gave 'em a pittance for the clock and then rang the cops, who managed to nick the little buggers.'

'So ... I'll get my clock back?'

The other three shared a grin and Dave said fondly, 'You will, Lib.'

Beside her, MJ patted her hand and smiled into her eyes.

From where she stood in the crowd, Libby saw a man on a cherry-red bay canter into view. As they approached the finish line, she glimpsed the prophet's thumbprint depression in the muscle of the bay's neck and gave a loud cheer. Raising an arm above her head she began waving, and a shaft of sunlight glinted red and white off the strikingly beautiful garnet and diamond ring on her left hand.

'And in fourth place,' the announcer said over the PA, 'we have local man Mitchell Johnson riding a mare he bred and trained himself, Cherry Red, by Australian Stockhorse champion Red Letter.'

After waiting for the applause to die down, he continued. 'Hearty congratulations go to both horse and rider for completing the course in the top five. I'm sure we'll be seeing these two at the next Tom Quilty, where they might even ride off with the coveted gold cup.'

When the rider spotted Libby his face broke into a broad grin. Beaming back at him, she pushed her way through the crowd, heading for the man she loved.

The man she was about to marry.

Mitchell Johnson.

MJ to his friends.

∼

If you've enjoyed THE LONG ROAD TO LOVING MITCHELL, I hope you'll consider posting a review on your retailer's site. Libby and Mitchell will love you for it!
Alicia :)

OTHER NOVELS BY
ALICIA HOPE

THE LONG ROAD TO LOVING JACKSON

It's said that bad things often happen in threes, but if a girl's lucky she just might be offered a second chance ... or three.

Confronted with a suspicious death, mounting farm debts, and a squatter she can't seem to shake, injured trick rider Abbey has some tough choices to make.

Cut and run or stay and ride it out?

Defy her uncle again or redeem herself?

Lower her guard or fortify her heart's defences?

On a long road it can be the hitchhikers we collect along the way that make the journey worthwhile.

The Long Road to Loving Jackson is available in paperback and as an ebook.

THE LONG ROAD TO LOVING GRAYSON

Uber-capable HR officer Maggie is in love, just not with the man she married - a situation she didn't anticipate ever having to face.

And when engineer Grayson travels to a remote Queensland town to relieve for six weeks, he doesn't anticipate having to summon the Flying Doctors, survive a tropical cyclone, or lose his heart along the road....

The Long Road to Loving Grayson is available in paperback and as an ebook.

THE CAFE BIRDS

A *literal* chick lit novel!

What does a girl do if she has a soldier husband suffering from PTSD? Or an abusive boyfriend, a recently Goth teenage daughter growing more distant every day, a callous and unfaithful life partner, or a guilty conscience and gluten intolerance keeping her from the man of her dreams? She calls up her BFFs and vents over coffee and cake of course!

A no-fail recipe: in five pretty cafés, blend women friends and their modern day dramas with to-die-for coffees and scrumptious cakes and serve.

Bon appétit!

The Cafe Birds is available in paperback and as an ebook.

MEET THE AUTHOR

Once you choose HOPE, anything is possible....

You can connect with Alicia online at
http://www.aliciahopeauthor.blogspot.com

www.ingramcontent.com/pod-product-compliance
Lightning Source LLC
Chambersburg PA
CBHW030618120726
47904CB00006B/1944